DREAM CHASERS AND
THE RIDDLE-SPOKENS

Manufactured under license granted to AMEET Sp. z o.o. by the LEGO Group.

AMEET Sp. z o.o.
Nowe Sady 6, 94–102 Łódź – Poland
ameet@ameet.eu, www.ameet.eu

www.LEGO.com

Published in the United States by Random House Children's Books, a division of Penguin Random House LLC, 1745 Broadway, New York, NY 10019, and in Canada by Penguin Random House Canada Limited, Toronto. Random House and the colophon are registered trademarks of Penguin Random House LLC.

rhcbooks.com

ISBN 978-0-593-48477-7 (trade) — ISBN 978-0-593-48478-4 (lib. bdg.)
ISBN 978-0-593-48479-1 (ebook)

MANUFACTURED IN CHINA

10 9 8 7 6 5 4 3 2 1

DREAM CHASERS AND
THE RIDDLE-SPOKENS

By Kaela Rivera

Random House New York

Contents

Prologue 1

Chapter 1: The Perfect Z-Blob 5

Chapter 2: The Art-scapade 17

Chapter 3: Into the Dream World 33

Chapter 4: The Many Poses of Z-Blob 41

Chapter 5: Gates of Fantasy 57

Chapter 6: Fight in the Square 69

Chapter 7: Captive Sister 79

Chapter 8: The Riddle-Spokens 89

Chapter 9: Into the Castle 99

Chapter 10: The Second Riddle-Spoken 113

Chapter 11: The Trapped Riddle-Spoken 125

Chapter 12: A Daring Plan, Stan 135

Chapter 13: Dream Siblings 147

Chapter 14: Team Tower 161

Chapter 15: Home Again 175

Chapter 16: The Art Show 181

Epilogue 195

Glossary 199

About the Author 211

Dream Journal 213

Prologue

Have you ever dreamed of a world where being unique and creative were superpowers? A world where magnificent places and fantastical creatures never cease to amaze an awestruck visitor?

What if you discovered that everything you see, feel, smell, and touch in your dreams is actually . . . reality? This wonderful world, filled with imaginative realms, is not as far away as you might think. In fact, many travel there every night, not long after they close their eyes and fall asleep.

As you have probably already guessed, the dream world is real. It is made of endless spectacular realms that look like floating islands in the sky. They are inhabited by mystical creatures created by the imaginations of people just like you. Yes, it's true.

Most people are regular dreamers—they may or may not remember their dreams—and don't suspect that everything they experience in their dream actually did happen. But among us, there are also aware dreamers. These dreamers know the dream world is no less real than the waking world. And they can participate in the dreams of others. When they are awake, they remember every detail. As you may have guessed, there are only few of these special aware dreamers.

The heroes of this story are aware dreamers. In the waking world, Mateo, Izzie, Cooper, and Logan are ordinary kids who live in an ordinary world and go to an ordinary school. But in the dream world, they have an extremely important job to do.

As regular visitors in the dream world, they discovered that while it may be filled with adventure, fantasy, and awesome experiences, it is also home to danger. The evil Nightmare King, with his dreadful army, plans to conquer the dream world.

Fortunately, the friends have help saving the dream world from this wicked enemy! The Night Bureau is an ancient, secret organization that maintains the fine balance between the waking and dream worlds. Mateo, Izzie, Cooper, and Logan have become members of the Night Bureau and are known as dream chasers. With the help of Mr. Oswald, their science teacher and an agent of the Night Bureau, some of the young heroes learn the power of dream crafting—the ability to create amazing objects, vehicles, creatures, and anything they can imagine in the dream world.

Now that you know the truth about the dream world, you can join these extraordinary heroes every night when you go to sleep. Just use your imagination and unique creativity to protect the marvelous dream world and sleeping children from the terrifying Nightmare King and his sinister forces.

Are you ready? Adventure awaits!

Chapter 1
The Perfect Z-Blob

Mateo got up extra early on a special Monday morning. Not for school, but to try to do something he'd never done before: create a drawing he planned—or maybe, hoped—to actually share with someone else.

Mateo was still just a teenager, but his dad sometimes liked to say he was an eighty-year-old artist in his head. Mateo wasn't sure about that as he bowed his head of thick brown dreadlocks over his stack of drawings all the same. He'd been drawing pictures of Z-Blob, his comic book character, as long as he could remember. But he never showed people his drawings. Mateo placed his free hand on his desk as he scanned the pictures he'd been working on. Were any of these good enough to let someone else see? He wasn't sure.

Mateo had been sketching for at least an hour before Izzie, his younger sister, suddenly yawned loud and proud behind him. He glanced back at her to find her sitting on her bed, dressed and sleepy but ready for school. Izzie shared his dark brown hair, but hers was long and wavy and fell down her back. But that was about where their similarities ended. Where Mateo preferred to wear calm blues and plain jeans, Izzie always looked like a rainbow had exploded on her clothes. And where Mateo was generally quieter, a bit introverted, Izzie lived like she was lightning incarnate.

Even now, this early in the morning, her eyes were already starting to sparkle with the excitement for a new day.

"We did such a good job last night in the dream world!" was the first thing out of her mouth. She pointed at him with her stuffed bunny. "You swooped in and totally kicked those nightmares' butts with your Z-Blob airplane! That was so clever, bro!"

Mateo shushed his sister, and gave her a look as he put a finger to her lips. He quickly checked to make sure their father couldn't hear through the door, then he locked it. Izzie covered her mouth and winked conspiratorially. Because they had a vital, world-shattering secret. Where most people thought dreams were just magical nonsense that you experienced while you slept, Mateo and Izzie knew better. They had discovered that they were aware dreamers—the dreamers who understood that the dream world was just as real as the waking world. When they fell asleep at night, everything they did in the dream world really happened. They could participate in other people's dreams, and unlike the unaware dreamers, they remembered everything when awake. In time, Mateo and Izzie also realized that the dream world was not quite a safe place. There was a wicked presence lurking in the shadows of the dream world—a powerful creature capable of stealing the imaginations of sleeping children. He called himself the Nightmare King. And he used the stolen imaginations to fuel his Nightmare Army.

Thoughts of the Nightmare King and his forces made Mateo shiver, so he tried to distract himself. "I liked that unicorn Bunchu you made last night," he told Izzie in a hushed voice. "Where'd you get that idea?"

She stood up on her bed, grinning. "Uh, the series finale of *Bunchu Bunny Kung Fu Rabbit*, the best anime of all time! I was just thinking, what could make my Bunchu even better? And boom! I knew it was giving Bunchu a unicorn horn!" She giggled.

Izzie had a talent for thinking of something one second and making it happen the next. Mateo turned back to his dozens of sketches and sighed. He'd been working on these for the past week, but he was finally running out of time.

"You'd know all that if you'd watched *Bunchu Bunny Kung Fu Rabbit* with me!" Izzie pointed at Mateo's bed. "Even Z-Blob loved it. Right, Z-Blob?"

Z-Blob was Mateo's comic book character, but ever since they first went into the dream world, this small, green, blobby creature had become a real, true friend. He came back to the waking world from the dream world with them all the time. Right now, he sat perched on the side of Mateo's bed, by his backpack. He straightened up when Izzie pointed at him and made bubbling, gurgling sounds in agreement.

Izzie gestured to her gelatinous friend. "I rest my case."

Mateo laughed "Okay, okay, I'll watch it with you after school. But I'm a bit busy right now. I have to finish something before we leave."

That got Izzie's attention. She leaned forward, rubbing her chin. "Homework?" she asked.

"No," he said. He shifted to better cover his papers. Mateo felt safe telling Izzie most things, but he kept his drawings even from her.

"Ooooh, then is it a *love letter* or something?" Izzie grinned. "Is it for Zoey?"

"What? No!" Mateo's cheeks flushed red. "Mr. Guerrero told me about this art competition coming up, and I was just trying out a few ideas to submit. That's all."

Izzie's eyes lit up. "Wait, really? You're going to enter to a real-life waking world art show with other people looking at your work and everything? Bro-seph, that's great!" She jumped up and down on her bed in excitement.

Mateo cringed a little. He hadn't meant to tell her, but the last thing he wanted was for her to think he was writing Zoey a love letter. Because Zoey was awesome. And she definitely seemed like the kind of girl who would be annoyed if he started spewing poetry.

"Show me what you're going to enter!" Izzie came rushing over. "I want to see!"

Mateo quickly covered all of his mashed-up paper balls and doodles.

"No! Don't look, Izzie!" he said anxiously. "It's not done yet."

Izzie stopped trying to peek around his shoulder and sighed. Slowly, Mateo straightened back up, gazing down at his drawings in the safety of his shadow. In Mateo's imagination— and in the dream world as well—Z-Blob could transform into anything. The new sketches showed his green friend as a flying car, a robot T. rex, and a mechanical wizard. None of them were what Mateo wanted. None of them were . . . perfect. Not yet.

Mateo normally couldn't stand people looking at his work at all. He'd shown classmates a few times when he was really young, but he'd stopped pretty quickly once they'd started to criticize his doodles or ask him to draw them instead. A few of them had even said his work looked dumb. After that, he'd kept his drawings almost exclusively to himself.

Mateo would not even have considered submitting to the competition if Mr. Guerrero hadn't accidentally caught him drawing.

"That's such good work, Mateo," he'd said. The compliment had rung in Mateo's ears like hope. "You should submit to the upcoming art contest!"

Mateo really looked up to his art teacher, even if he only showed him his work sometimes. Mateo could trust Mr. Guerrero. But other students? Anyone and everyone in the school would be invited to come look at the art in the competition. And someone would be assigned to judge their work. To sit there and criticize his drawing it in front of everyone his age.

The thought nearly made him nauseous. If Mateo was going to submit to a competition, his work had to be completely, 100 percent perfect. He could only imagine how much people would laugh and make fun of him if he didn't get it all right.

Izzie finally flopped back down on her bed. "Well, I'm still stoked you're going to submit something everyone can see. You're so good at drawing! And I bet Mr. Guerrero will be super excited to see you enter. He really wanted you to join art club at the beginning of the semester!"

Mateo had almost taken Mr. Guerrero up on that offer to join the art club—but to be part of the club, everyone had to submit an art piece every week and then have everyone critique it. Mateo hadn't been ready for that. And now he had dream chaser duties, and that kept him plenty busy in the waking world as much as the dream world.

"I don't think I can submit," Mateo said quickly. Izzie lifted her head with the first signs of concern. "The deadline is today, and I told myself I'd only enter if I could come up with something really great by this morning. And I haven't."

Izzie shook her head. "No way! You've got a pile of drawings there—can't you just pick one? All your stuff is really good!"

Mateo could never *just* do anything with his art. That was the problem.

"You talk like you've never seen my art," he pointed out.

"I know your art and I know you," she said, with way more confidence than Mateo could ever understand. "You're really good."

With a sigh, Mateo stood up and started putting his drawings away. Izzie made frustrated, worried noises the whole time, but he was used to her making a lot of noise, so it was easy to ignore.

"Mateo—" she started.

"I just don't think I'm ready." Mateo paused to look over all his scribbles. That's all they were. No matter how many hours he poured into them, none of them seemed to transform from scribbles to true art pieces. "None of these are good enough, Izzie. Maybe . . . maybe I'll try next year."

Izzie pouted. "That's what you said last year."

"Mijos!" a voice called from downstairs. "Time for breakfast! Come on, you'll be late for school!"

Mateo snapped out of all his worried thoughts and quickly tucked the last of his drawings away into a folder and then into his backpack. Izzie threw him his books, and he tossed her favorite pencils into her bag (she always forgot them if he didn't). Then he held out the half-open backpack toward Z-Blob, who nimbly jumped inside. Just as he was leaving the room, Izzie hesitated by her brother's desk.

"What?" he asked.

She lifted a piece of paper. "The art contest form. You're really not going to enter?"

Mateo played with his backpack's straps. After a moment, he sighed and kicked his sneaker against the carpet. "No, I'm not ready yet. My sketches are still sloppy, and I haven't figured out what the perfect version of Z-Blob to submit would be."

"But—"she started.

"I mean it, chicos!" their dad called again.

"Coming, Papá!" They returned and ran out the room.

But what Mateo didn't see was Izzie hesitating behind him for a few moments in the room. Or the way she slid his blank submission form into her backpack as they left. Or the smug smile on her face as a new idea brewed in her head: a way, she was sure, she could get her brother to take the leap and believe in himself as much as she did.

Chapter 2

The Art-scapade

Later that day, Mateo was headed to lunch when he spotted the art room. He paused in front of it, staring at the call for submissions plastered on the teacher's door.

ART-STRAVAGANZA! NEXT FRIDAY AFTERNOON, ALL CLASSES WILL BE RELEASED TO REVIEW AND CELEBRATE THE WINNERS OF OUR SCHOOL'S ART COMPETITION. LEAVE STICKERS BY YOUR FAVORITE ENTRIES AND RECOGNIZE OUR SCHOOL'S GREAT ARTISTS.

Mateo's heart sank a little. These flyers had been plastered across the school advertising it for weeks, and most people Mateo knew were excited to get out of class and look at art instead of having to do schoolwork for an hour. It was a good thing he'd decided not to submit. He was surprised he'd even considered it seriously. If there was anything worse than having someone judge his artwork, it was having the whole school come and see how imperfect it was in comparison to everyone else's. Mateo wasn't sure he could have ever lived down the humiliation.

Mateo looked up past the flyer and up at Mr. Guerrero's name on the art room door. Even if he was relieved to avoid his classmates seeing his work, he did feel bad about letting Mr. Guerrero down.

Mr. Guerrero had purposefully pulled him aside a week ago and invited him to submit. Would his teacher be disappointed? But then again, Mr. Guerrero was a *real* artist. And Mateo was certain none of his sketches would live up to all Mr. Guerrero's expectations anyway. Sure, he'd complimented some of Mateo's doodles when he'd noticed him working on them in the lunchroom, but Mateo was nothing compared to a real master.

Mateo was just about to turn away when the door to the art room swung open.

"Mateo!" Mr. Guerrero appeared in the doorway.

Mr. Guerrero had warm eyes and a cheerful, loud voice that made his mustache quiver whenever he talked. Normally, Mateo would be happy to see him. But today wasn't a normal day.

He smiled weakly. "Hey, Mr. Guerrero. Good to see you."

Mateo was already trying to come up with an excuse for not submitting something when Mr. Guerrero chuckled merrily.

"I was so happy to see that you entered the art show, Mateo! I'm excited to see your work. Just remember to drop it off by tomorrow after school, okay? I don't mind giving you an extension, but we'll still need time to do the judging before the big ART-STRAVAGANZA later this week."

Mateo froze. His stomach felt like it had dropped to the floor.

"Is there a problem?" Mr. Guerrero asked.

"Sorry—did you just say I'm in the art show?"

"Of course!" Mr. Guerrero pulled out a piece of paper and offered it to him. Mateo's insides tightened when he saw his name scribbled at the top. "Your sister came by earlier with your entrance form. She said you were too busy to drop it off this morning and forgot your art piece. No rest for the busy artist, eh, Mateo?"

Mateo's entire body went cold. His stomach did a tap-dance on his gut, and for a second, he was afraid he'd be sick. Wordlessly, he watched as Mr. Guerrero went back into the art studio, saying something positive he couldn't hear, and carrying the form Izzie had obviously forged.

Mateo gaped. Izzie didn't have the same issues with showing her work that he did. And she was always super supportive about his stuff, even if she didn't usually sit still long enough to hear about it.

But Mateo had never thought Izzie would do something like *this*.

Mateo began to panic. He wasn't ready for an art show. He wasn't ready for anyone besides Z-Blob to see his work, and he definitely wasn't ready for a ton of people to see and *judge* it, or for the discouraged way Mr. Guerrero would look at his amateur work. His backpack shuddered on his shoulder, and Z-Blob peeked out at him, as if he sensed his distress.

"What am I going to do?" Mateo asked him. He set off down the hall. Slowly, the fear turned to anger. *"Izzie, how could you do this to me?"*

Mateo found Izzie at lunch, sitting with Cooper and Logan. Cooper was Mateo's oldest friend. He had blond hair, perfect grades, and perfectly crisp, bright clothes. Sometimes Mateo wished he could get everything as . . . well, as perfect as Cooper did. But Cooper's real talent lay in following instructions; that's what made him a science whiz.

Logan, on the other hand, was just about the opposite. He was Mateo's first real bully, and for some reason, Cooper had become friends with him just before they'd all discovered that the dream world was real. Logan had a wide, too-confident grin most of the time, along with a shock of black hair, a backward baseball cap (like he was reminding everyone how cool he was), and a loud voice perfect for mocking "art dorks" like Mateo. Mateo would absolutely hate the fact that Logan was a dream chaser, like he, Izzie, and Cooper were—except that Logan wasn't always so bad. Once, Logan had even helped Mateo prepare for their school's sports day. He hadn't expected that. But it had shown him there was a bit more to Logan than he first thought.

Against all odds, he, Izzie, Cooper, and Logan had become dream chasers together, protecting the dream world from the Nightmare King. Most days, it made Mateo pretty happy to see them all there at the lunch table, waiting for him. It reminded him he wasn't alone.

But today was different. They were all just chatting as if everything was fine, while Mateo's life had just been sent flying into fiery turmoil. Mateo stomped his way over, heart beating in his ears, ready to confront Izzie. His sister spotted him and waved excitedly at his approach. For a second, his heart floundered. She looked so happy to see him.

But then Mateo remembered the ART-STRAVAGANZA, and all that was left inside him was fear and anger.

"Hey, Bro-seph—" she started.

He cut her off as he stopped beside her. "How could you do this, Izzie?"

The excited smile fell off her face. Cooper leaned over her, his blond hair swaying.

"Hey, is something wrong, Mateo?" he asked.

Logan laughed. "Yeah! Your face looks like a tomato or something."

The heat in Mateo's face only intensified.

"That always happens when he's mad," Izzie mumbled, clear concern growing on her face.

Quickly, she tried to replace it with a sheepish smile. "Um, I'm guessing you talked to Mr. Guerrero?"

"Yeah I did!" he said, and slammed his backpack down on the free seat beside her. "Izzie, I told you I wasn't ready! And you forged the form! That's so messed up!"

She cringed. "I know, I know! But your drawings are so good, Mateo! I just want you to be able to share them with everyone."

"But I told you how I was feeling, and you just ignored me."

"That's because you can't see how awesome you are, so I did it for you! You need to stop overthinking so much," she said, smiling wider, like she was hoping his anger would lessen. But it was only getting worse the more she pushed. "Like when we're in the dream world! You gotta let go and just let yourself feel it. Right, Cooper?" She looked behind her. "You know how much he holds himself back!"

If Mateo was embarrassed and scared before, the shameful feelings doubled when Cooper looked up at him and gave a sheepish shrug in agreement.

"You've been working on Z-Blob comics and illustrations as long as I've known you, Mateo," Cooper said. "It would be good if you could finally finish one of them. Share it with other people. What else are you going to do with them?"

"But she forced me into it!" Mateo said. "Now Mr. Guerrero's expecting something from me that I don't have. I only have sketches! Nothing I want to show the entire school at the ART-STRAVAGANZA that every single class will be coming to. I'm not ready!"

Izzie's black eyes widened. "Wait, the whole school is coming to the art show?"

Mateo slapped the flyer down on the table. "You didn't even read it, did you? What am I going to do now, huh, Izzie? Just get humiliated in front of everyone?"

"Yeah, that is pretty uncool, Izzie," Cooper added.

"Well . . . I . . . Um . . . I didn't realize . . ." Izzie trailed off.

"Can you ask for an extension?" Cooper asked, ever the problem solver.

"Today was supposed to be the due date. Turning something in by tomorrow *is* the extension!" Mateo's heart was tightening into a stone again. He could barely breathe. "This is all your fault, Izzie."

She gaped. "But I was just trying to help! I didn't think that—"

"Exactly!" Mateo burst out. "You never *think*! And now I'm the one that has to pay for it!"

Izzie's face fell. Cooper grimaced as the words echoed across the broad lunchroom and the nearest five lunch tables near them quieted. Even Logan stopped smirking at the fight long enough to look uncomfortable.

"Dude," Logan said. He rubbed the back of his neck. "Bit harsh."

The last person Mateo wanted to hear criticism from was *Logan*. With all the insults

Logan threw at him for no reason, Mateo deserved the opportunity to get mad at least once, especially after Izzie forced him into this situation. He turned, ready to defend himself, when a new voice interrupted.

"You guys okay?"

Mateo looked up. Zoey had stopped on the other side of their table, lunch tray in hand. Mateo froze.

Zoey was an aware dreamer, too. She'd visited the dream world long before the others, and she liked to patrol it on her own. She was known there as the mysterious dream bandit who would cause mischief and steal precious items from the Nightmare Army to help innocent dreamlings and misplaced dreamers. She was cool in the dream world, but she was possibly even cooler in real life. Mateo had a hard time not staring in wonder whenever she played her guitar. Her short, coiled black hair would bounce as she strummed, and her serious dark eyes were as sharp as stars in the night sky. Um—not that

Mateo thought about how pretty her eyes were that often.

Now, she stood across the table from him in her all-black outfit, eyebrow raised. She never ate with them at their table, but she always sat nearby. She must have been on her way over to an empty table when she overheard their argument. Usually, Mateo was happy to see Zoey. He wanted a chance to get closer to her. As friends. But right now, while he was panicking and anger was rampaging in his heart, he was more humiliated than ever. He didn't want her to see him like this any more than he wanted every class in school to see the dumb sketches in his backpack.

Mateo snatched up his backpack. Z-Blob peeked at him from the unzipped insides.

"Nothing's wrong," he said. His cheeks and chest were hot, and he couldn't look Zoey in the eye. "I just have to figure out how to handle this on my own now. Thanks for nothing, Izzie."

Mateo turned, stomping away to who-knew-where, his mind whirling. Should he just tell

Mr. Guerrero he had to withdraw from the competition? Tell him what Izzie did, that it was a mistake? But then, Mr. Guerrero had looked so proud of him. And he'd already added the form to the others, already added Mateo's name to the list of contestants. The only thing more embarrassing than showing everyone his work would be telling them he was too scared to share his work.

He couldn't back out. But how was he going to create the perfect piece of art between now and tomorrow? Mateo hung his head as he walked to the lunchroom's exit, his stomach hollow and empty.

But as he reached the door, he couldn't help peeking back at Izzie. She had her head bowed over the lunch table, squeezing her hands together, looking sadder than he'd seen her in a long, long time.

Chapter 3

Into the Dream World

Mateo and Izzie didn't speak for the rest of the day. Not between classes, and not on their way home, and not at dinner. Even their papa noticed.

"You're so quiet. . . . Something happen at school?" he'd tested.

Izzie folded her arms, pouting. Mateo stared sullenly at the carne asada and frijoles on his plate. He wanted to talk about it. But he didn't know how. He was afraid if he talked about it again, he might burst like an ugly volcano, the same way he had at lunch. Eventually, their dad gave up and it was time for bed.

Or rather, for dream chasing.

Mateo and Izzie dressed in their pajamas without a word to each other. Mateo listened to Izzie's noises as he crawled into bed and pulled the covers around himself.

Izzie broke the silence.

"I just wanted to help," Izzie whispered to him, once she was in bed. She wiggled in her saber-tooth tiger pajamas. "You're so creative, Mateo. You should share your talent with other people. It'll make you a better artist! Like the ones who draw Bunchu Bunny Kung Fu Rabbit!"

Mateo tried hard not to say anything so he didn't explode again. But here his sister was, making more and more excuses for herself. She didn't get what it was like, did she? Izzie didn't have a hobby she cared about. Half the time, Mateo didn't think Izzie cared about anything. All she did was watch anime and play with stuffed animals, and today, make his life harder.

"I don't get why you're so mad," Izzie said. "I mean, sure, the whole school seeing something you're not ready to show isn't great, but just think how much cooler it'll be when you totally win and surprise everyone! Even yourself!"

Mateo squeezed his eyes closed and tried to will himself into the dream world. Unfortunately, it didn't work like that. Even if he was a dream chaser, he had to fall asleep to enter the dream world, just like everyone else.

"I can help you brainstorm more ideas, too, if you want!" she said. "I've got your back——"

Mateo finally snapped.

"You wouldn't have pushed me into this if you really had my back! I can't believe you haven't even apologized for it!" Mateo rolled over to glare at her. "And you know what? You don't get why I'm mad, because unlike you, I actually *care* about how the stuff I create turns out. Every time you try to draw something in the waking world, you abandon it before you finish because you get distracted. And sometimes you can't even keep your stuff together in the dream world because you don't stick with it long enough! Remember that time you got distracted and then your giant Bunchu turned back into a tiny stuffed animal? You nearly fell down a mountain!"

Izzie tucked her plushie Bunchu to her chest. "That was one time. I'm not that bad."

"You are so, Izzie! You think I just need to just 'stop overthinking,' like it's that easy? Well— maybe you should think more about how what you do affects other people!"

Izzie's bottom lip crumpled. She rolled over, turning her back to him.

"Fine," she said. "Be mad at me. I'm mad at you now, too. I don't even want to watch *Bunchu Bunny Kung Fu Rabbit* with you anymore!"

"Well, I don't want to, either," Mateo said.

"Fine!" she yelled.

"Fine!" he yelled back.

Mateo winced, though. He'd promised to watch it with her, and he didn't like breaking his promises.

It was really hard falling asleep after that.

But dreams can't be resisted for long. And slowly but surely, as the light waned and their room was soaked in the navy blues and grays of night, Mateo and Izzie fell asleep—and entered a familiar world of wonder and power.

When Mateo opened his eyes, he was in the dream world. Logan and Cooper were already there, waiting for him and his sister on the dream landing.

The dream landing was the dream chasers' safe space in the dream world. A large green floating island, with a blue tree house in the middle, surrounded by beautiful, sparkling mists filled with warm colors. They each had a bed waiting for them. Mateo sat up, waiting for his friends to come over. He looked at the glowing doors around him. He knew that once a door opened, they would fly through it and be transported into other realms in the dream world.

"It's about time!" Logan popped up in front of Mateo. "We've been waiting for you. What took you so long?"

Cooper elbowed him. "Dude."

"What? I'm just asking what took them so long—"

Cooper dropped his voice to a whisper. "Do you even remember what happened at lunch?"

"I don't remember anything longer than I have to," Logan proclaimed proudly. "Keeps all the energy going to my muscles."

Logan flexed. Cooper sighed.

"Is Mr. Oz here yet?" Mateo asked.

Mr. Oz was the dream chasers' teacher both in the waking world and in the dream world. It had surprised Mateo, too, when he'd seen his science teacher in the dream world for the first time. Especially since Mr. Oz traded his usual tucked-in shirt and glasses for a long lab coat and hard-core eye patch in the dream world. He looked like a mad-scientist pirate. But as a member of the Night Bureau, the secret organization that kept the dream and waking worlds separate, Mr. Oz had been able to show them everything they needed to know about surviving here and fighting nightmares. Including the all-important skill of dream crafting.

Mateo pulled out his hourglass. He and every one of the dream chasers had one, besides Logan—he'd failed his trial to get an hourglass. Although many dream chasers didn't need an hourglass to dream craft, without one it was almost impossible to keep focus and control the dream sand that created what the dream crafter imagined. Complicated dream crafts consumed more dream sand, but Mateo had plenty of it in his hourglass right now, since it was the beginning of the night. He'd be able to create all kinds of things here in the dream world with it—when he felt confident enough. He wished it was as easy to do that in the waking world.

"Not yet," Cooper said. "No sign of Zoey yet, either. But she does things on her own time, I guess."

"If she does show up, though, I'm ready." Logan whipped a pair of sunglasses out of his pocket. "See what I brought?"

"You brought . . . sunglasses? From the waking world?" Cooper asked.

"Izzie brings her toys, so I thought I should bring something actually awesome."

Mateo stared harder at his dream sand. And it gave him an idea. A brilliant, fun, wonderful idea that he thought just might be an answer to his problems.

If Mateo couldn't decide on a drawing of Z-Blob in the waking world, he'd just dream craft them here until he found the perfect pose to submit to the competition!

Chapter 4
The Many Poses of Z-Blob

The best thing about the the dream world for Mateo was that here he could experiment as much as he wanted without any nosy strangers at school seeing (or rather, remembering) if he failed or not. So taking time in the dream world to come up with the perfect pose of Z-Blob was the perfect solution to his problem. Maybe that way he would not completely embarrass himself once he woke up and had to finish something he would submit for the ART-STRAVAGANZA competition. Because of you-know-who.

Mateo glanced across their floating island and found Izzie clutching her Bunchu plushie, grumbling to herself as she paced in front of a nearby door to another realm. Should he say something to her? Mateo had never really seen Izzie mad.

He turned around and strode to the center of the landing, pulling out his hourglass. No— he wasn't going to be the first to reach out, not when she still hadn't apologized. Anyway, he was busy now. He had to figure out how to create the perfect Z-Blob, and now he finally had a chance.

Mateo pulled out his hourglass and lifted it up. "All right, Z-Blob!"

Z-Blob leapt up onto his shoulder. *"Squrp?"*

"Yeah, we're going to try something out. Ready, buddy?"

"Squuirr!"

Z-Blob leapt off Mateo's shoulder. And before he could even land on the lush grass, Mateo lifted his hourglass, pictured something in his mind, and focused as hard as he could. Light glowed from his hourglass. The hourglass shivered, golden light drifting from it and surrounding Z-Blob. Z-Blob's whole body disappeared into the light—and slowly began to transform as the sand swirled around him.

Finally, Z-Blob rose as a giant cyborg, with rocket fingers, legs that looked like skyscrapers, and Z-Blob's jiggly body as a head, fitted with an extra-cool robot laser-eye. Mateo grinned. That wasn't so bad. But—his smile dropped—could he call it perfect? No, something was still off.

That was okay. Mateo had lots of cool ideas; he just had to pick the right one. Quickly, he dream crafted a new idea, and Z-Blob's body transformed in glowing, sunny streaks, until he stood as a giant gladiator with a futuristic-looking sword. Hmm, but was his stance right? Maybe the futuristic gladiator was cliché now? Mateo dream crafted again and again. Z-Blob turned into a race car with robot arms, a plane with steam-powered engines, and then a giant metal lion with a detachable drone head.

But none of it looked perfect.

None of the versions looked like they would win a competition. The judges would laugh at him. Or worse—tell him he wasn't good enough to be a real artist.

"Hey, Mateo, don't you think you're wasting a lot of dream sand?" Cooper remarked.

"Dude!" Logan jumped on Z-Blob's giant metal lion foot. "Now make him a building, and I'll climb him like King Kong!"

Mateo frowned. "I'm not playing around, Logan, I'm practicing! I only have until tomorrow to submit something for the art competition, and it's gotta be flawless."

Logan folded his arms but didn't get off the foot. "It's all about 'perfect' with you. Look, I don't even have an hourglass to get things all perfect, and I can still dream craft. Kinda."

"You turn into a small blue goblin," Mateo said, arms folded. "That's not the same thing."

A while back, Logan had been held prisoner in the Nightmare King's lair. During his escape, he had learned to transform himself into a small blue version of himself (but with bigger teeth). It was the closest thing to full-on dream crafting he'd done his whole time as a dream chaser. Mateo had been impressed that he could do it all without an hourglass, but it wasn't nearly as powerful as what he could've done with one.

"I said 'kinda'!" Logan jumped off Z-Blob's foot and headed for Mateo. "Look, dude! The point is, you can't always get things right, and you've just got to accept that. You can still do cool stuff without being perfect. Right, Coop?" Logan asked.

Cooper looked a little stiff. "Uh, um . . . I don't know about that. My parents get pretty upset if I don't get things right the first time."

"Exactly." Mateo knew Cooper would get it. Cooper was so . . . perfect about schoolwork, presentations. Dream crafting was about the only thing that he didn't ace right away. Mateo turned back to Z-Blob. "Now come on, guys, I've got to focus."

"Whatever." Logan huffed and walked off. "Where's Mr. Oz? Even he's more fun than you right now. . . ."

Mateo ignored that, but Cooper stepped up and watched as Mateo tried to decide what to dream craft Z-Blob into next. What would impress the judges? And Mr. Guerrero? And more important, what would keep him from being mocked by other students? He didn't want to hear what they'd say if he couldn't get this right.

Cooper awkwardly patted his side and looked over at Izzie. "So I'm assuming you two still haven't made up?"

"She totally tried to force it on me," Mateo said. "That's not cool."

"I agree with you, man," Cooper said, with an understanding nod. "It's just—" He looked away and sighed.

Something about that sigh was different from his others, as if he was about to say something important and difficult at the same time. Mateo lowered his hourglass and let Z-Blob return to his original form. Cooper rubbed the back of his neck.

"What is it, Coop?" Mateo lowered his voice. Cooper didn't usually struggle to speak. He was acting—well, not perfect.

"I have siblings too, you know," Cooper mumbled. "Two older brothers who are so great at everything that no matter what I do, I'm not good enough for them. Izzie's younger than you, and yeah, she's pushy, and she didn't respect that maybe you're creative in a different way from her. But I don't know, man." He looked up. "I just can't help but think it would be nice to have a sibling who believed in you that much. I wish just one of my brothers cared as much about me as Izzie does about you. Then maybe I wouldn't feel like I was one mistake away from being a failure all the time."

Cooper tried to say it nonchalantly, but his voice broke a little on the last sentence. Mateo's angry insides faltered as he stared at his long-time friend. They'd grown up together, and Mateo had never heard him admit that before.

Cooper was scared of being a failure, too? That was news to Mateo. Cooper was so smart, always had his day scheduled, always had his homework done, and never shied away from presenting in group projects. He'd always seemed like he had his whole life together already. Mateo had always thought that if Cooper had been an artist, too, he probably would have already won like ten art competitions by now.

"No one's perfect," Cooper murmured. "That includes your sister. Maybe try to talk it out?"

Mateo found himself looking Izzie's way. She was frowning to herself, sitting on the opposite side of the dream landing from him, all her usual spark deflated. Izzie had always tried to help him. But what if she kept doing things like this? Why was she so focused on changing him? He didn't try to make her change. Well, he didn't usually. Before tonight.

There's a difference between supporting someone and trying to remake them. And what Izzie did felt way too much like the latter.

But before Mateo could decide what that meant, and what he should do about it, the roaring of a jet pierced the air. Mateo and Cooper tilted their heads back and watched a flying vehicle appear in the mists surrounding the dream landing. The aircraft was quite large, with a bright yellow school bus for its main body and long white wings with massive jet engines on both sides. That was Mr. Oswald, all right. And his school-bus-jet kicked up wind across them all as it neared.

"It's about time, Mr. Oz!" Izzie called out. "Time to go on an adventure!"

Of course that was her first thought. Mateo crossed his arms and frowned as the jet rumbled overhead, slowly lowered, and finally rested on the green grasses of their dream landing.

The jet's door hissed and popped open to reveal Mr. Oz standing there, ready. "All right, everyone!" he called out as he wandered down the ramp. "We have a very special mission today. Rumor has it that Lunia's been spotted somewhere in the Fantasy Realm. Now, I don't need to tell you how important that could be for us—"

"I will," a voice with a Southern accent interrupted. A chimp in an astronaut suit popped his head out the pilot's window.

"Albert!" Everyone cheered.

The chimp smiled and waved to them. He was Mr. Oz's long-time dreamling friend, the way Z-Blob was Mateo's.

"Lunia's the strongest dream crafter that's ever been, and the only person strong enough to put the Nightmare King away again and save the dream world! If she's back, we need to find her ASAP," Albert continued, and then pointed at them. "Before the *Night Hunter* does."

The Night Hunter. Mateo almost shivered thinking about the nightmare-stained hunter who was always hot on their heels. He was the Nightmare King's head minion, dedicated to helping the evil king take over the dream world and spread nightmares across the whole of it.

He wouldn't be satisfied until he'd captured every dreamer and used their imaginations to help him snuff out all the light and joy of the dream world.

It was their job as dream chasers to make sure that never happened.

Mr. Oz sighed. "Like Albert says. Now, come on, all of you! We're headed to the Fantasy Realm! The unicorn migration is soon, and we don't want to get stuck in that traffic. . . ."

Izzie had been pacing, stroking her Bunchu plushie, but at the mention of unicorns she stopped dead and suddenly whirled around. "Did you say *unicorn migration?* I haven't seen unicorns since we first arrived in the dream world!"

"Yes, yes. And if the Nightmare Army is on its way to follow the Lunia rumors, like we think it will, we need to get there fast." Mr. Oz strode down the bus-jet's ramp. "By scaring the unicorns, they could turn that migration into a stampede. That will put tons of dreamers in danger, and if Lunia is in the Fantasy Realm, we could lose her trail in the mess and panic."

Mr. Oz made some great points, but Izzie wasn't listening. The moment Mr. Oz described the endangered unicorns, she was already hurtling herself in the direction of the nearest door. It opened as she pushed toward it. The swirls inside began to glow with stars and rainbow light.

"I have to save the unicorns from the nightmare creatures!" she cried, right as she leapt toward it. "And the dreamers! They need me! I'm coming for yoouuuuu!"

Izzie vanished through the portal, leaving everyone gaping after her. Before anyone made a move, the door slammed shut. Then it grew smaller and . . . disappeared. Mateo slapped a hand to his forehead.

Izzie was fearless—and tended to jump into things without thinking. But it always got worse when she was stressed out, which he had to guess she was, considering they were fighting. Great.

That meant she'd be even harder to reason with until they tried to patch things up. But why was it always Mateo's responsibility? Just because he was older than Izzie?

Mr. Oz bowed his head. "That girl. Oy. All right, everyone, come on." He gestured back at the jet. "We got to go catch up to her before she gets herself in trouble."

"Shotgun!" Logan shouted to claim the front seat for himself. He sped up the ramp. "Do you think they have dragons in the Fantasy Realm? I want to ride one."

"You're not a ninja, Logan." Cooper followed him inside.

"Come on, Mateo. We need to get to your sister," Mr. Oz called. "You don't want her to be in danger all on her own, do you?"

Mateo trudged up the ramp. "No," he said. "Of course not."

Chapter 5

Gates of Fantasy

The jet hummed along, cutting through swirls of pink and purple clouds as the team traveled through the vast and endless dream world. Mateo had only been to a few parts of the Fantasy Realm, back when they were enduring their trial in the Dream Forge to get their hourglasses. He turned his hourglass in his hand, watching the lights of the jet flicker across its glass curves. He and Izzie had gotten through that trial together. As brother and sister, they had gotten through everything in their lives together—bad grades, difficult news in the family, and even becoming dream chasers.

Mateo's heart ached a bit as he watched the dream sand shift around in his hourglass.

"Everyone's pretty quiet today," Mr. Oz remarked. Mateo shook himself and straightened up in his seat. "Well, good. I'm gonna hope that's because you're focusing really hard on our mission, preparing your minds for what's coming. You know the importance of Lunia as the only person ever to defeat the Nightmare King. And you'll all need to be on your toes in the Fantasy Realm."

Everyone pretty much ignored Mr. Oz after that, though he didn't know it. Albert sighed up front as Mr. Oz gave a rousing speech that the rest of them talked through.

"This just doesn't feel the same traveling without Izzie, you know?" Cooper mumbled to Logan and Mateo.

Logan raised his eyebrows. "You mean because we can actually talk about something besides nerdy stuff like *Bunchu Bunny Kung Fu Rabbit?"*

"Hey, lay off," Mateo snapped in the seat behind him.

Logan turned around in his chair. He wasn't wearing his seat belt—again. "What? You're the one who's mad at her!"

"She's still my sister," Mateo snapped, and slumped in his chair. Even when he was mad at Izzie, he still loved her. She had been by his side basically all his life, and she had always been a ray of sunshine that seemed to push back the clouds of his heart on hard and difficult days. No matter what their family went through, she was looking for the bright side.

Mateo's heart softened a little, as he gazed out the jet's window. He actually admired Izzie's strengths. Out of their whole team, she was probably the most fearless, on par with Logan but way more creative. Sometimes Mateo even wished he could be a bit more like her. It would be so much easier if he could do like she said and just not overthink. If he could suddenly master his mind and no longer be afraid. But he wasn't like Izzie. He worried all the time about what people would say about the things he created. She'd never experienced what that was like. The looming, nightmare-like fear that others would laugh or mock your work—or worst of all, tell you that it was so bad, you should never create again.

"Well, it's not like she can't take care of herself," Logan said, and shrugged over the seat. "She can dream craft even faster than you." He pointed to Mateo's hourglass. "And she's got more dream sand than you right now, after you used up so much of yours for all that art competition stuff. I don't get why you're so in your head about it. You draw all the time. Just pick something and submit it! That's what I do on tests."

Cooper laughed. "No wonder your grades are so bad."

Mateo's cheeks heated up. "I don't want to pick some random thing, Logan. I want to pick the *right* one! Because if I don't—" Mateo stopped himself before he admitted the fear out loud. He didn't want to tell Logan how afraid he was of having people judge his work. Possibly laugh at it. Possibly scoff.

"I get what you mean, Mateo," Cooper admitted. "You may not feel it, Logan, but it can be a lot of pressure to try and get stuff right the first time." He frowned.

Logan waved their concerns away. "Who even cares, though? It's not like anyone important pays attention to art contests anyway."

Mateo rolled his eyes.

"Okay, everyone!" Mr. Oz called out. "We're getting ready to land at the gate of the Fantasy Realm!"

"Logan, your seat belt—" Albert started to say.

The whole jet rocked, and Logan went flying across the jet and into the nearest wall. Mateo muffled a snicker, and Cooper winced.

"Logan, just use the seat belt." Cooper rolled his eyes.

"You can't . . . tell me . . . what to do!" Logan groaned where he lay crumpled on the ground by the door.

"I can give you detention tomorrow," Mr. Oz offered.

"Seat belt it is!" Logan leapt up.

"Now focus up all of you," the chimp said. He unbuckled his own seat belt, and Mateo, Cooper, Logan, and Mr. Oz met him at the doors. They readied their hourglasses, all gleaming with dream sand. "This part of the Fantasy Realm has all kinds of wild creatures in it. Our goals are to get Izzie, search the area for Lunia, and stay out of the way of the Nightmare King's army. Got it?"

"But don't be afraid to fight if you need to," Mr. Oz reminded them.

"Yeah, yeah, let's go!" Logan rubbed his hands together. "I want to see some man-eating monsters!"

The doors of the jet opened. And as they stepped out, they were surrounded by the wild, wonderful, colorful world of the Fantasy Realm.

"Whoa," Mateo breathed.

Before them, the Fantasy Realm rolled out in castle towers stretching toward a blue sky streaked with bright, brilliant pinks, like the sun was rising beyond the cotton-candy and mushroom trees surrounding the large, glistening city. There was a set of wide, powerful gates just separating them from the rest of the fantastical land, made of rainbow-welded crystals. Distant silhouettes flew through the sky. But were they fantastical dreams and beasts—or nightmares?

"How are we going to find Lunia in all of this?" Logan asked.

"Or Izzie?" Mateo asked.

"Wherever Lunia is, some of the greatest dream crafting will be also!" Mr. Oz said. He adjusted his belt and stepped toward the Fantasy Realm's open gates.

But before any of them could get very far, a low, familiar jingling sounded to their left. Mateo, Logan, Cooper, Mr. Oz, and Albert all turned to find Mrs. Castillo—the fun older lady who sold burritos in their neighborhood—sitting in her traveling turtle shack named Señor Tortuga—as it slowly, ever so slowly, made its way to the giant entrance gate. She was just putting up her shop when she noticed them and waved. Mateo almost laughed. Mrs. Castillo had a knack for appearing out of nowhere, even in the dream world.

"Hello there, chicos!" She motioned them forward. "Would you like any magical items from my pawn shop? Perhaps a hat that will make you fly? Some new pencils for you, Cooper-ito?"

"No thank you, Mrs. Castillo," they called out to her together.

Mateo ran toward her and stopped in front of her cart. "Actually, we're looking for my sister, Izzie. Have you seen her by any chance, Mrs. Castillo?"

Cooper and Logan stopped beside him. "Or Lunia?"

"*La luna?* Hmm, I did see a very beautiful moon earlier tonight," Mrs. Castillo said.

"No, Lun-*i*-a," Logan sounded out.

Mrs. Castillo smiled and shook her head. "I have not seen that, either. But I *can* see very clearly that you all look very impatient to get to your destination, eh?"

Mateo certainly was. He had to get to Izzie, then they had to complete their mission, and then he had to figure out how to finish an art piece in the morning—and fast.

"But you know, creativity is not a linear thing. Your journey may go up and down, and it may be slow and long or fast and short. What matters is that you press forward on your journey, step by step." She reached down and patted Mateo's dreadlocks. "So try and let go of what you think you must have or must be, mijo."

Mateo brushed his dreadlocks back down after she'd ruffled them. What she'd said felt important—but also super unhelpful right then. They were on a mission. And if it was important that his art competition submission was perfect, then it was ten times more essential that this went off without a hitch.

"She's really on another planet from us, huh?" Logan asked on the corner of his mouth.

Mrs. Castillo pointed off. "Anyway, chicos, it looks like that might be your next step on your journey, sí?"

Mateo turned—and his stomach knotted into a ball. Before he could see anything, he felt a rumble in the ground. Like a thunderstorm of hooves rattling through the stones and the trees. And then, just beyond the entrance gates of the Fantasy Realm, a stampede of metallic, shining unicorns tore out of the forest. Mateo gasped. He, Cooper, and Logan whirled around. Mr. Oz readied his cannon.

Because it wasn't just a mindless stampede. It was a battle, and the herd of unicorns was trying to escape some truly nightmarish pursuers.

Izzie rode the unicorn at the head of the galloping herd. Their horns pierced the wind. The frightened girl was looking back, her hourglass out, as the Night Hunter and a pack of grimspawn—nightmare creatures made from

the imaginations of captured dreamers—chased her.

The Night Hunter looked their way once, his black-and-hot-pink glare cutting beneath his large, broad hat. He cackled beneath his bandana, turned, and urged his army to quicken their pace.

Chapter 6
Fight in the Square

Izzie, the pack of shining unicorns, and the flying horde of nightmares were already almost out of sight, headed toward a distant city of castle towers and fairy-tale cottages. Mateo led the whole group as they rushed toward the gates. But no matter how fast they ran, it wasn't enough to keep up.

"They're too fast," Mr. Oz said. "The jet's not prepared for hot pursuits. We need something better. Time for some dream crafting, kids!"

"I'll make a drone out of Z-Blob!" Mateo said, and pulled out his hourglass.

"No, Mateo!" Mr. Oz pushed his hourglass back down. "You're already low on dream sand. You probably have only two dream crafts left. You've got to conserve it!"

Z-Blob, perched on Mateo's shoulder, gurgled sadly. Mateo's heart plunged. Of course, Mr. Oz was right. He shouldn't have spent so much time overthinking the Z-Blob poses earlier. However stressed he was about the art competition, his responsibilities as a dream crafter were too important to jeopardize like that. Dreamers and the dream world were relying on them to keep the Nightmare King at bay.

Logan jumped forward. "Coop! What about that thing you've been practicing?"

Cooper's eyes lit up. He pulled a toy car wheel out of his back pocket and eyed it. "A car could definitely keep up with a herd of unicorns, right?"

"Now we're talking!" Mr. Oz said. "Gather round, kids. Cooper, go on. You got this. Just remember not to overthink it too much. Let it flow."

Cooper struggled to dream craft more than Mateo and Izzie because he had difficulty imagining something without instructions. But he focused on the toy wheel, analyzing it so carefully Mateo could nearly hear matching gears turning in his head. Cooper was excellent at focusing. As long as he could get out of his own way long enough, they'd be zooming in no time.

Cooper closed his eyes. "Just don't overthink it," he whispered.

Mateo's stomach clenched. That was Izzie's saying. Ever since she first told it to Cooper, he'd used it as a sort of mantra to relax and allow his imagination to flourish.

And flourish it did.

Mateo stepped back with Logan, Mr. Oz, and Albert as light encompassed Cooper. It stretched out from the simple toy wheel, transforming, enlarging, until Cooper sat at the steering wheel of a large red car equipped with a little silver flag at the back and seats enough for all of them.

"Get in!" Cooper grinned.

Mateo and Z-Blob got inside first, but Logan took shotgun anyway. Mr. Oz fitted his laser cannon to his shoulder and peered through the eyeglass. Albert swung into place beside him and Mateo.

"Step on it, Cooper!" Mr. Oz called.

The car's wheels kicked up a cloud of dust—before they shot straight down the path and through a tunnel of tall cotton-candy and mushroom trees, focused on the distant sound of hooves. Z-Blob almost flew off Mateo's shoulder with the speed, but Mateo grabbed him and held him close.

"Our first order of business is helping Izzie fight off the nightmares!" Mr. Oz said, over the roar of the engine. "They definitely heard the rumors of Lunia and came here looking for her, but they won't leave the unicorns alone until we get them out of sight."

"So we need to evacuate the unicorn migration?" Mateo asked. He stood up, peering over the seats, checking the horizon for Izzie. Right then, streaks of forest and magical animals were all he could see.

"What about looking for Lunia?" Logan asked.

"We can do that as soon as we've solved this issue," Albert interjected. "Safety first, kids. You can't search for someone if you're being shaken awake by a nightmare!"

He had a good point. And to make his point even better, a flash of darkness suddenly leapt in their way—a stray unicorn, being ridden by a cackling grimspawn with large yellow teeth, crooked wings, and eyes like fire. Cooper yelped and took a hard left to avoid hitting them.

"*AHHHH!*" they yelled.

Cooper lost control of the car. It started to spin around, its tires screeching while making donuts in the sand. Mateo clung to the seat and cried out. Z-Blob splattered against the back seat. Mr. Oz and Albert clutched each other, screaming. Logan, fortunately, actually had his seat belt on this time, so he only got winded as the car finally spiraled into the fairy-tale town square.

The town square was large, with a tall blue-and-white crystal tower to the north. It was so tall, Mateo almost couldn't see the top, except for a small red-and-green dot that implied a shingled roof covered with lush ivy. On their left and right were cottages and mushroom houses of all different shapes and colors, all of them bright and cheerful. But the sight directly around them was a lot less cheerful.

Their car was surrounded by a herd of metallic, holographic unicorns on one side, and a whole pack of grimspawn on the other. In the middle, at the center of the town square, Izzie stood with her hourglass glowing, and her Bunchu plushie transformed into a giant living version of itself. She sat on it now instead of a unicorn, but she rode Bunchu as if it was just as majestic. She pointed at the Night Hunter, who was laughing at her.

"Leave these unicorns alone!" she yelled. "They're precious dreams, and you have no right to steal them!"

The Night Hunter just strode forward, shaking his head as he continued to laugh. "Silly girl. We're not here for the unicorns. But I'm not one to turn down an opportunity to please the Nightmare King. He wants all the dreams, and all the dreamers, he can possibly get. One day soon, his nightmares will outnumber you all."

"Yeah-hah-ha we will!" One grimspawn leapt forward, between the Night Hunter's legs. Mateo recognized him: Snivel, one of the grumpy little grimspawn always heading up the army.

"Maybe it'll even be tonight!" Sneak, a cat-shaped grimspawn with one bulbous eye, grinned beside Snivel. "How's stupid are you, anyhow? Coming out here all alone? You think we'll let you find Lunia first?"

"Shut up you two!" Susan, the smartest grimspawn kids had met, hissed. "Don't tell her about the rumors!"

So, they were here searching for information on Lunia, too. The Night Hunter yelled at the three of them before spreading his arms. The whole horde of grimspawn around him fluttered and cackled, readying themselves to attack. Except Sneak, of course, who curled up in the Night Hunter's shadow. He always seemed to find a way out of direct fighting.

Izzie's face, for the first time, grew worried as the horde eyed her. Mateo unbuckled his seat belt, secured Z-Blob on his shoulder, and flipped out of the car.

"Izzie!" he called. "Evacuate the herd!"

Her eyes lit up as she turned and spotted him. "Mateo! You came!"

Why was she surprised?

Mateo frowned as he ran up toward his sister with Z-Blob bouncing on his shoulders. Cooper, Logan, Mr. Oz, and Albert were hot on his heels. Cooper even started evacuating some of the unicorns, and many of them sprinted away into the forest for safety.

"Of course I came!" Mateo yelled. "We were *supposed* to go together! So this"—he pointed at the approaching nightmares—"didn't happen!"

Izzie grinned sheepishly. "Right, sorry. But the moment I heard unicorns, I couldn't just stand by and wait for the nightmares to get here first!"

A grimspawn flew for Izzie's face while she wasn't looking. Mateo ripped out his hourglass and the pencil he kept in his belt at all times. In one great flash of his dream sand, the pencil extended, enlarging into the size of a spear. He sent it flying—and it slammed into the flying grimspawn. It tottered in midair and screeched as it retreated.

"That's just an excuse and you know it, Izzie! You *could* have resisted if you tried! But you got impatient!" Mateo called out as he ran closer.

Izzie's face fell. She stared at Mateo, gripping Bunchu's fur nervously. And Mateo's heart pulled in a thousand directions. Because he wasn't sure what was harder or scarier—fighting with his sister, or all the nightmares surrounding them, ready for war.

Chapter 7

Captive Sister

Mateo skated to a stop in the square with Z-Blob and picked up his pencil-spear. He'd just saved Izzie from a nightmare's blow. But his hourglass was dangerously low now, the glitters of dream sand just barely coating the bottom. He had maybe one dream craft left. Mateo cursed himself quietly. He shouldn't have wasted so much earlier! Why had he let his fears rule him like that?

"Mateo—" Izzie started as she leapt down from Bunchu. Bunchu's edges began to shimmer, coming apart, as she faced him. She was getting distracted. "I know you're mad, Bro-seph, but I was just trying to help."

Two flying minions zipped toward their faces. Z-Blob gurgled a warning, and they barely dodged back in time to avoid their creepy claws.

"Guys, focus!" Cooper leapt in from their right. He pulled out a giant tire he must have dream crafted when they weren't looking. "This is serious! Help me with this!"

Mateo, Izzie, and Cooper all shoved at the giant tire. It rolled forward with unnatural speed, chasing down a pack of squawking grimspawn. Mr. Oz, Albert, and Logan were already fighting the rest after evacuating almost all the unicorns. Izzie high-fived Cooper.

"Nice! Your dream crafting gets better and better, Cooper!" She lifted her fists. "Now let's take on all these baddies! I'll just get on Bunchu and . . . Oh!"

They turned and found the magnificent steed Bunchu now reduced back to a plushie. It lay on the ground, motionless, waiting. Izzie gasped and scooped it up against her chest. She must have gotten too distracted and let the dream craft unravel.

"Oh no!" Izzie said. "Bunchu!"

A laugh rocked the square. Mateo whipped out his giant pencil, pointing it at the Night Hunter. Izzie scowled at his approach. Z-Blob curled up menacingly. Mr. Oz was busy reloading his laser cannon. Logan, now in his blue goblin form, rolled up imaginary sleeves like he was going to charge right for him. Albert grabbed at him to talk him down.

"I don't know why we bother to consider you enemies," the Night Hunter called out to them. "This little girl can't even maintain her dream crafts because she's too excited about unicorns, or too chatty with her brother, hah!" The Night Hunter snapped his fingers. "So you might as well get out of here. We have an important mission today. We can always capture you tomorrow night."

"Over my dead body!" Izzie shook her fist.

"No need for that," the Night Hunter said.

Mateo's head was nearly busting. They were on an important mission, too—they shouldn't have been on this tangent of a fight to begin with. In fact, they wouldn't even be at risk, half surrounded and fighting in this town square, if it wasn't for Izzie once again pushing where she shouldn't.

"If we'd come together, this wouldn't have happened!" Mateo suddenly snapped and rounded on Izzie. "You never think things through! You didn't wait for us to search for Lunia together, just like you didn't wait for me to submit my own art application! You have to stop pushing things onto people, Izzie!"

The Night Hunter blinked. "Um—excuse me, I'm trying to threaten you over here."

The siblings weren't paying attention to him. Izzie's eyes caught the light as she met Mateo's eyes. Tears edged her lashes, and she squeezed her hourglass tight.

"I know, Mateo!" she confessed. "I know I don't think things through! I'm impatient, and I'm pushy. That's why I admire you so much! You're so thorough and thoughtful and—cool! You come up with awesome plans and always help me focus. I probably couldn't even finish my homework without you."

Her bottom lip trembled.

"I guess—I guess that's why I hoped I could help you, too, if I could help you push past overthinking and share your art." Her eyes blurred with tears. "But I didn't help you. I made it worse. Just like I've done here. I—I'm sorry."

Mateo had been waiting for that apology all day. He knew Izzie meant every word. Almost instantly, his heart softened, and he regretted yelling at her so much. Izzie was just . . . trying her best. The same way that he was. They weren't really all that different, like he'd thought. They just had different flaws, different things that they struggled with.

Izzie was trying to help, even if she was misguided.

Across the square, the Night Hunter was clearly annoyed that he wasn't being paid attention to. He huffed.

"Sure, that's fine, just have a heart-to-heart while I'm trying to monologue at you." He whirled around and directed his minions to Mr. Oz, Albert, and Logan. "But I'm going to drive you out of here one way or the other! I'm walking away with Lunia today!"

"He knows about Lunia," Izzie whispered. "This is all my fault. If he finds out everything we know . . ."

Mateo reached over and touched her shoulder. She looked up with those big eyes he'd grown up with, and he whispered, "Izzie, I'm sorry. I—I didn't realize . . ."

He slowly reached out his other hand. Her bottom lip still trembled, but she reached for him in return. Before they could grab onto each other, a black-and-hot-pink streak dove from the sky like a flash and caught Izzie by the back of her clothes.

"Mateoooo!" Izzie cried helplessly as a pack of grimspawn stole her away.

"Izzie!" Mateo sprinted after her.

Mateo reached out for her hand again. Their hands scraped once before she was lifted higher into the air. Mateo could feel the warmth of her skin as he stared up into her wide, still-remorseful eyes. He tried to close his hand down around hers—but the grimspawn were too fast.

Mateo chased after her even as she grew farther away, still reaching for her. "Let go of my sister!"

But a laugh came from far above his head. Mateo looked up and found the Night Hunter crouched in the window at the top of the high, high tower. The grimspawn were flying a fighting, wrestling Izzie up toward him.

"So you wanted to find Lunia, too, huh?" the Night Hunter asked. "Well, then, I'm going to grill you until you tell me everything you know about her location. Don't bother fighting!" he crowed. Izzie fought anyway. "Resisting the might of the Nightmare King is pointless!"

"Mateooo! I'm sorryyyyy!" Izzie called out.

Her distant body vanished into the top of the tower, and the window sealed shut behind her, the Night Hunter, and the minions of the Nightmare King.

Chapter 8
The Riddle-Spokens

Mateo was desperate and furious. "We have to follow her!" he cried.

With Z-Blob readied, he charged for the tower, Cooper and Logan following him. Logan didn't even protest on the way. But before they could barrel in through the tower's heavy metal doors, Mr. Oz and Albert cut in front of them.

"Whoa, now," Albert said. "Just stop for a second there."

"That's my sister!" Mateo said. "I have to get her back!"

"Sllurugrp!" Z-Blob protested as well.

"Of course, of course!" Mr. Oz said. "No one's arguing that. But you need to be prepared before leaping inside like some wild devil-may-care hothead."

Albert nodded. "Like someone I know."

Mr. Oz glared at him just for a second before returning to Mateo and pointing back at the tower. "That's one of the most secure, dangerous towers in the whole Fantasy Realm," Mr. Oz said, focused and determined. "It's not going to be easy, you know. It's guarded by Riddle-Spokens."

"Riddle-Spokens?" Cooper asked. "What're those?"

"Powerful mythical beasts that could destroy you! They were said to be dreamed up by a deeply powerful dream chaser in the past." Mr. Oz pointed at each of them, to drive the point home. "Either way, you can't fight them head-on. The only way to get past them is to answer their riddles correctly, to offer some wisdom in return for their cleverness. Otherwise, they'll eat you and send you back to the waking world before we can rescue your sister."

"And I hope we don't need to remind you how important it is that you and your sister don't wake up while you're in danger in the dream world," Albert said. "You could bring something treacherous back with you, and in the waking world, a nightmare will be even more threatening than it is here."

Mr. Oz nodded. "You'll have to be extra careful and extra creative to make your way through the tests of powerful judges like these."

Mateo clutched his giant pencil-spear. Z-Blob leaned into him to offer courage. Mateo's heart beat like a drum in his chest, but he didn't care how scary the Riddle-Spokens were. If they were standing between him and his sister, he'd face them all.

"Then that's what I'm going to do!" Mateo said. He marched forward, toward the tower's doors.

"Mateo!" Albert called. "The rest of the Nightmare King's army is on its way. You have to be fast! Oz and I will do our best to buy you time, but you four need to be as fast as you can."

"You five, you mean," a new voice interjected.

They all turned and found a blue rush of wings alighting down on the ground. Mateo's chest lit up. Zoey, mounted on her giant blue cat-owl gryphon, Zian, nodded down at them all. Her face was cool as ever—but he'd heard what she'd said. She was coming with them.

"Zoey?" Mateo asked. "How'd you know to come?"

She patted her gryphon. "Zian. She could smell there was something wrong." She gazed out at the pink and purple towers, the flying animals zipping through bright cotton-candy clouds. "Plus, I heard about the Lunia rumors. Figured you guys would show up here, thought I'd come. You always get yourselves in trouble on your own." She pointed. "Then I saw Izzie getting carried off. Figured I was right to show up."

"I thought you didn't work in teams?" Cooper asked.

Zoey folded her arms and frowned. "I don't.", Zian cawed and prodded her with her black beak. "Well, except for Zian," Zoey amended, and stroked her blue feathers. "But—you know. I, uh. Owe Izzie a favor. Yeah, I'm just paying her back for it, tit for tat. That's all."

Mateo stepped forward, brandishing his pencil-made weapon. He was low on dream sand. Nervous about the tests waiting inside with powerful judges who'd weigh his every word. Still aching over his sister's last apology. But he wasn't about to falter, or overthink, or sit paralyzed by his fear anymore.

"Then let's go get my sister back," he said, and led the group inside.

The grimspawn dumped Izzie through the window and onto the floor of the uppermost room of the sealed tower. She yelped as she rolled across the ground, clutching her Bunchu plushie and hourglass. The Night Hunter entered much more gracefully and strode across the floor, cackling quietly as the grimpsawn gathered around him like a dark, fearful cloud.

"Well, now, we've got the noisy one," he said. "If you want me to leave your precious brother and friends alone, I suggest you tell me everything you know about Lunia. I heard you mention her. I heard you say you didn't want me to know something about her, hmm? Spill it, kid."

Izzie pushed off the ground, holding her precious items to her. She glared, humphing, eyeing the room. It was a wide, cylindrical area, with rafters far above her and a chandelier hanging from them. There was only one window behind the Night Hunter, framing his large hat, where he stood crowded with his nightmare minions. There were random items spilled about the room—pillows, strange sci-fi-looking tools, and more—like a bunch of forgotten dreams. This wasn't going to be easy, that was for sure.

But she'd already let her brother down once today. Okay, maybe twice if you counted the whole going-ahead-for-the-unicorns thing. But she wasn't about to do it again.

"I'll just dream craft my way out of here!" she called. "What're you going to do about that?"

The Night Hunter laughed. "Oh, yes! Go ahead, then. I'll just take your Bunchu like I did your—what did you call it? Mr. Sharky Jaw?" He snorted at the name.

Izzie's insides burned with horror. Mr. Sharky Jaw was her most cherished plushie that she once took to the dream world. During a fierce battle it was dream crafted by the Night Hunter into a huge, terrifying shark vehicle. When Izzie returned to the waking world, she found Mr. Sharky Jaw in tatters. He and Bunchu were very precious to Izzie. She squeezed Bunchu tight to her chest. Any dream crafting plans she had must avoid using her plushie this time.

"Didn't think your way through this one, did you, little dream crafter?" The Night Hunter folded his arms, and the grimspawn cackled on either side of him. "Now, I need to know. How much do you know about Lunia's location?"

Izzie's brain cranked up. She wasn't used to making plans. But she tried to focus, did her best to take in her surroundings and think through her options. Like Mateo would do. She needed to buy herself time and figure out how to get out of this place.

The Night Hunter didn't realize she didn't know anything about Lunia's location. Mr. Oz hadn't said much about the rumors, and even if he had—she, uh, hadn't stuck around long enough to hear the rest. But if she could keep the Night Hunter's focus on her instead of the rest of the team, she could keep them safe until she figured out how to escape and get back to them. It was a win-win.

If she could figure it out, anyway.

Izzie's hourglass brightened. She would figure it out. Mateo was right. She wasn't good at focusing, and now the Night Hunter was relying on that to get his way. But Izzie was never one to back down from a challenge, either. So she'd have to do her best today to strengthen her weakness. If she could just think like Mateo for a bit, be a bit more patient, she could hold the Night Hunter off long enough with dream crafting to either figure out a way to escape—

Or wait for her brother and friends to help her out.

"How much do I know about Lunia's location?" Izzie frowned and scratched her head. She needed to stall for time. "Well, I can talk about Lunia for hours, but I bet you'd rather see this cool trick I can do. . . ."

Chapter 9

Into the Castle

The inside of the tower didn't look anything like the shining, white-and-blue, crystal-covered creation on the outside. The insides were narrow, and Mateo had to turn sideways sometimes to keep following the blue wooden stairs up in a winding pattern. Z-Blob even stretched himself tall and thin to make sure he didn't get caught on anything. Zoey followed quickly after Mateo, and they all finally reached a hallway they could stop to breathe in after about ten minutes of climbing.

But Mateo didn't want to stop and catch his breath, even as he panted and could barely stumble forward.

"Whoa, Matty," Logan said, and Mateo glared at him for the nickname. "You got to pause a second and breathe. Take it from someone who rocks race days."

Mateo nearly rolled his eyes, but Logan was definitely the better athlete of the two of them. "I can't just stop! I've got to get Izzie. I—I need to tell her I'm sorry, too."

"Wait, you two haven't made up yet?" Zoey balked.

Out of everyone he knew, Zoey was the last person Mateo wanted to see him looking petty. Especially when she looked so cool and—he coughed—a little pretty in her dream bandit outfit. She lifted her eyebrow suspiciously.

"Well?" she asked.

Logan wedged his way in. "Yeah, he's still mad at her. Guess he's not as mature as us cool, level-headed types." He grinned at her.

Zoey completely ignored him. "I don't get it. What is it about the art competition that's so important to you? I've never seen you two fight. Why's it such a big a deal to you?"

Unlike the way Logan had asked way back in the lunchroom, Zoey's question, though hard and sharp, was also sincere. She really wanted to know. Mateo paused on the steps.

"I'm not as mad anymore. And it's not just the art competition," Mateo slowly confessed. He looked around their group and let out a shaky, calming sigh. "The thing is, ever since I was a kid, all I can remember wanting to do is draw. I want to make my own comic book and share all the cool ideas and stories in my head. I tried once, and kids made fun of me. Ever since then, it's like I care about it so much that I can't . . . I can't seem to do it. Not in front of anyone, anyway."

"You're scared," Zoey offered.

Mateo met her dark eyes. Mateo had never thought Zoey would be familiar with fear at all, let alone fear that felt this big and hungry. But the look in her eyes implied otherwise. Zoey's expression was a little distant, a little somber. Like she recognized the kind of fear he was experiencing. The kind of fear that comes when you care about something so deeply. The kind of fear that steals away the thing you loved in the first place.

"Izzie is not like me in that way," Mateo continued more quietly. Even Logan was listening now—not interrupting, just listening, actually focused, actually invested. "When she cares about something, she goes after it like a firework. I guess I was even more mad that she was the one who'd pushed me into a situation I was scared of. Because I knew she didn't know what it was like. But . . ."

"No one's actually fearless," Zoey whispered. Mateo looked up, surprised.

"Just like no one's actually . . . perfect," Cooper added. He was looking away dramatically, as if an old fear of his was lurking back up in his mind, too. "Trust me. I know"

Mateo gazed from one to the other. Maybe his friends had bigger struggles than he thought. Slowly, he nodded. Zoey folded her arms, humphing a bit, and pushed up the next couple steps.

"Well," she said. "Let's go show those Riddle-Spokens that you're not about to let them scare you into giving up something else you care about. Right, Mateo?"

Mateo straightened. "Right!"

As soon as Mateo finished climbing the steps, his fellow dream chasers rallied around. The narrow stone hallway came to an end with only a red-and-gold door left to pass through. The first Riddle-Spoken. Mateo took a moment to calm his breathing. Slowly, he reached up to knock on the door. Logan let out an exaggerated sigh and pushed forward, sending Mateo stumbling to the side. Z-Blob wobbled on his shoulder before righting himself.

"Hey!" Mateo said as he patted his jelly friend.

"You're taking too long! I got this." Logan puffed up his chest and knocked on the door.

The rumble was followed by dreadful, heavy silence. Logan looked confused. A bit more slowly this time, Logan raised his hand to knock again. But then the door opened, by itself. Beyond it, there was nothing but darkness. Logan frowned a little.

"Huh," he said. He peeked a little beyond the doorframe, looking a tad nervous. "Did Mr. Oz lie to us? I don't see anything." When nothing happened, he dove his head in farther, the nervous look vanishing with a cocky grin. "Eh, well, I guess this'll be faster anyway—"

Suddenly, a large silver chain flashed out from the door. Logan yelped, and Mateo dove for him as the chain wrapped around Logan's middle. But there was no time to save him before the chain whisked him inside, beyond the door, into the darkness. Logan's scream faded in the black mists.

"Logan!" Mateo yelled unison with Cooper and Zoey.

They dove into the room after him.

At first, it was nothing but mists and smoke. Mateo coughed and fanned the air in front of him as he pushed into the room. Z-Blob shuddered. Cooper called his name. Suddenly, Zoey grabbed his hand. Mateo's cheeks flushed.

"Hold on to each other," she called out. "So we don't get separated!"

"Coop?" Mateo called.

Cooper's hand grabbed his jacket from behind. "I'm here! But it's so dark, I can't see anything. Where are we?"

"An excellent question . . . ," a voice echoed out from the darkness.

Mateo froze, hand in hand with Zoey and clutching Cooper, as two silver eyes sparkled up in the darkness. The smoke cleared around them, and a giant snake made of metal feathers shone above them. Mateo gasped as its slithering, feathered body wrapped around them, trapping them in a circle at the center of the cloudy room. Its sparkling eyes narrowed on them.

"I am the first Riddle-Spoken, the Feathered Beassssssst," the serpent hissed. She had a high, silky voice, and her body made metallic tinkling

sounds as she moved her head left and right to peer at them. "To pass beyond my room, you must first passssss my test."

"What about Logan?" Cooper called. "Where is he?"

"Thissss one?" the snake asked. Her body tightened around them, her metal feathers making the sound of wind chimes. Slowly, the end of her tail came into view, and Logan dangled from her grasp, his mouth covered with feathers. "He is a recklessssss, thoughtlesssss boy. My perfect prey. But you will receive him back, should you succeed."

"And if we don't?" Mateo asked.

Her tongue flickered out her mouth. "You will see. Are you prepared to be judged, adventurersssssss?"

Mateo swallowed. If there was anything he hated, it was exactly that—going into a test he wasn't prepared for. Putting his creativity to a test, being judged. Failing. But Logan and Izzie were both on the line now. So he straightened up proudly, summoning all his courage, and nodded.

Zoey folded her arms resolutely. "What's the riddle, Feathered Beast?"

The serpent's smile widened. It had clearly been years since anyone challenged her, and she was excited to make it worth the wait.

"I deceive you by promising my path is faster, but I make sure you can never finish your journey," she said. "I let you run as fast as you can, but give me my way, and you may never get any closer to your goal. What am I?" The snake's eyes flashed. "You have ten secondssss to answer."

Ten seconds? That wasn't long enough! Mateo's heart beat in his ears as he searched his brain. What let you run without getting closer to anything? What could promise you a fast path and never let you finish a journey? His mind roamed, frantic. But it reminded him of something, didn't it? Something Izzie had said earlier. She'd used a specific word. It was on the tip of his tongue—

"Time'ssss up!" the Feathered Beast cried.

"No, wait!" Cooper said.

Zoey pulled out her bow. "You'll have to go through us first!"

The giant serpent looked ready to do just that. She struck forward, her mouth wide, fangs out. Mateo's mind whirled, searching for the word, as she sprang to swallow him whole.

"Impatience!" Mateo burst, and threw up his pencil-spear. "Impatience is the answer!"

The snake's mouth paused, her fangs still craning over his head. Slowly, she drew her head back. A new twinkle entered her eye, and she waved Logan in the air until the smoke cleared, and they could finally see the bright open window and the wide, circular room they stood in. Just behind the serpent, a new door appeared, bright blue and waiting for them.

"That issss correct!" the Feathered Beast hissed. "It is impatience that promises a quick creative journey and robs it out from under you. Congratulationsssss, adventurerssss." She dropped Logan free of her grasp. "You may continue on, victorioussss."

"We did it!" Mateo cried. Z-Blob jumped up and down on his shoulder, feeling victorious, indeed.

"That was awesome, Mateo!" Cooper cheered. "Impatience! Of course!"

Logan shuddered and rubbed his arms down. "Really cut it close there. But you saved me, man." He reached out a fist to bump. Mateo paused. Then smiled as he bumped knuckles back. "Thanks, Mateo."

When Mateo looked up from the congratulations, Zoey was already at the blue door across the room. She gestured for them to follow with a quirk of her head.

"Come on," she said, with just a hint of a smile. "We've still got more Riddle-Spokens to beat."

Chapter 10
The Second Riddle-Spoken

Unlike the first Riddle-Spoken's room, the second one's was filled with light. It was so bright, in fact, that Mateo, Zoey, Cooper, and Logan all had to block their eyes with their hands and shuffle forward warily. Z-Blob warbled a bit in discomfort as they pushed into the room. Mateo squinted, but the light never dimmed. His eyes even watered, it was so hard to look forward.

"Oh, wait!" Suddenly, Logan pulled out his sunglasses and placed them on his face. He grinned at them. "Check these out. They're cool *and* functional. Not such a waste to keep these babies around, now, was it?"

Mateo had to close his eyes against the light. "Can you just tell us where the Riddle-Spoken is? Or—"

Suddenly, the floor beneath them rumbled with giant, heavy footsteps. Mateo tripped into Zoey, and she pushed him upright. He didn't even have time to be embarrassed before a giant golem with a bright lantern for a head stopped in front of them. The creature was twice as tall as either of them, with a large round stone for a stomach and sharp quartz crystals for fists. Mateo could barely see, but all the light seemed to be coming directly from the golem's lantern. Looking up at him was like trying to look directly into the sun.

"Adventurers!" the golem said. Well, more like yelled. He was so loud, in fact, that they all trembled and slapped their hands over their ears—except Logan, who just peered up at him through his sunglasses with a grin. And Z-Blob, of course, who didn't have ears. "You have made it to the room of the second Riddle-Spoken. I am the Stone Golem. Are you prepared to face a momentous question that, if you should fail to answer to my satisfaction, will mean you will be thrown out my window at once?"

When they nodded, the Stone Golem slowly lowered the brightness of his face. Mateo, blinking rapidly to recover from the light, peeked sideways. There was a very large window there, with plenty of room for them all to be thrown out easily. He winced a little. If they fell out from here, they were sure to wake up—without Izzie. His heart hammered. That couldn't happen.

Zoey let out a long breath. Mateo glanced at her. Her face was tense.

"We can do this," she told Mateo, in barely a whisper.

Mateo stared at her for half a heartbeat. Was Zoey—scared? She was always so brave and strong and cool. She looked at him when he didn't answer right away. Her eyebrows rose, and she looked nervous, even though she frowned.

"Are you scared, too?" he asked.

Zoey scowled. She stumbled over her words for a second, but as the Stone Golem stopped in front of her, she froze. He craned his lantern head down to look at her. She bristled as she stared into his bright candle.

"Well, adventurers?" he asked. "Are you prepared to lose everything?"

Zoey didn't blink as she stared into the golem's hard, blinding lantern.

"I've already lost everything once," she said. She stood straighter, lifting her chin. "I'm not going to lose it all again. We have a friend—er, ally—to save."

And that's when Mateo was certain: Zoey *was* scared. She wouldn't need to be so brave if she wasn't. And even though Mateo's heart was shuddering in his chest, he somehow felt safer, comforted, to know he wasn't the only one afraid.

"Is that so?" the golem asked Zoey.

Mateo stepped up beside her, meeting his lantern in the eye—or candle, to be more accurate. He laid a hand on Zoey's shoulder.

"That's right," he said. "Give us your best shot, Stone Golem!"

"Oh-ho! Get ready, then!" The Stone Golem laughed a rattling, earthquake-y laugh. He straightened up, placed his crystal fists on his hips, and looked down at them. "Who is the captor of inspiration?" His voice rumbled, and everyone cringed as his voice shuddered through the floorboards and the rafters far, far overhead. The golem squatted again, so his lantern head looked Mateo right in the eye. "Who fills the mind with so much smoke that there is no more room for light?"

Man, these riddles were killer. Mateo's mind spun again as he looked from the golem's lantern to the window to the roof. What captured inspiration? What filled minds with smoke so there wasn't room for light? He squeezed his eyes shut. The Stone Golem shivered.

"You have twenty seconds," the Stone Golem warned.

Z-Blob made a bubbly protesting sound.

"Yeah, what he said," Logan said. He scratched his chin at the golem. "Are you sure you're not going to eat us like the snake lady? You're all just trying to get a meal out of this, aren't you?"

"Of course not," the Stone Golem said simply. He shuddered again, but this time, his stone body began to shake apart into large rocks. Zoey pulled Mateo out of the way, and all four of them plus Z-Blob all put their backs together. The Stone Golem's boulders surrounded them in a perfect circle. Each one shivered. And suddenly, they weren't just boulders. Each one sprouted a small lantern head and sharp, cutting crystal fists and feet. The mini golems narrowed their flame eyes and pointed sparkling, spiky fists right at them. "I'm a golem of my word. I will grab you all and throw you out the window. Ten more seconds left!"

Mateo's heart pounded, and for a second, he couldn't think at all. What had the question been? Something about inspiration? What steals inspiration? Mr. Oz talked about inspiration a lot, but it was hard to remember what he'd said with a sharp quartz fist leveled at his nose.

"You're running out of time," the mini golem in front of Mateo said.

Zoey's back pressed into his as the golem in front of her stepped closer. "You're going to lose," the mini-golem said.

All the golems took a step closer, their rocky laughter shaking the room. They closed them into a sharp, stony circle, pressing in inch by inch. Mateo scrambled for an answer, but how could he think when his brain was so crowded with fear?

"Wait! It's like what you two were saying out in the hallway, right?" Logan asked.

For a second, Mateo was so surprised Logan was volunteering something useful that he forgot to be scared. But Cooper gasped.

"Wait, Logan's right!" he said. "Zoey, Mateo, it's what you both were saying—"

Zoey grabbed his shoulders. "That's it! Mateo, it's—"

"Fear," Mateo said as the realization settled on him.

The mini golems' hands froze inches from their faces. Mateo, squished against his friends, peeked over Zoey's shoulders. She was holding her breath. Silence bloated in the room and hung over them like spiderwebs.

After a moment, the golems shuddered. Slowly, they began to leap back onto to each other, assembling back into the giant they'd originally met. Zoey grabbed Mateo's hand, just for a second, and squeezed. He breathed a sigh of relief.

The Stone Golem rose back into the giant creature that had first greeted them. Once back together, the massive stone golem took off the top of his lantern head and, using it like a hat, tipped it at them with respect.

"Excellent work!" he said. "You must be very brave, to know fear so well." He patted Zoey's head, and she looked both annoyed—and a bit relieved. "Did I spook you all?"

"Uh, yeah, man!" Logan said. "Not cool! I don't want to be smashed up, got it?"

The golem chuckled good-naturedly. He was actually pretty cheerful when he wasn't threatening their lives. "Of course, of course. Sorry, it's part of the job. This tower was made by a very powerful dreamer when she was young, you know. We're designed to be good bodyguards."

Zoey whipped around. "Wait, a powerful dreamer? Do you mean Lunia by any chance?"

"Oh, yes indeed. It's been a long time since she visited." The golem scratched his cheeks and looked to the wide window. "I was just cleaning out some of her old things yester-night, actually. I was sad to see them go, but then, space is at a premium when you're as big as us Riddle-Spokens."

Cooper sighed. "Oh, man. That's probably the rumor Mr. Oz heard about, then."

Zoey folded her arms. "It was just some of her old stuff being thrown out the tower. She's not here after all."

"Oh, is that what you're in our tower for?" the golem asked.

"No," Mateo said. "Well, I mean, that would've been nice. But we're actually here for my sister. The Night Hunter stole her and has her trapped up at the top."

The golem straightened. "He broke in? Oh, dear, that means he beat the third Riddle-Spoken. Perhaps she got distracted cleaning again. She has a problem with that."

His little flame eyes blinked down at Mateo.

"You certainly must move on quickly, then, hmm? Family is the most precious thing you could ever want to protect." The golem popped the top of his lantern back on. "Congratulations, adventurers. You may now pass on. And when you meet the next Riddle-Spoken, tell that fastidious sculpture to focus! Getting distracted on the job, *hmph* . . ."

Mateo couldn't help but laugh. Z-Blob bounced and gurgled on his shoulder, too. The Riddle-Spokens might be a bit scary, but they weren't bad.

The golem stepped to the side and gestured behind himself. There was a red door hanging from two chains. It wasn't set in a wall, so Cooper immediately ran up to investigate it. He peeked behind it, under it, and went all the way around it before shrugging as they walked over.

"It doesn't go anywhere," he said.

The golem laughed. "Of course it does! It leads to the last Riddle-Spoken. And if you get past her, you'll reach the top of the tower."

Cooper knocked on the door. It swung on the chains. "But—how?"

Zoey grabbed the doorknob. "This is the Fantasy Realm, remember, Cooper," she said, and pulled the door open. "Stay on your toes, everyone! We're going in."

Chapter 11

The Trapped Riddle-Spoken

When they opened the red hanging door, there was a large open room visible inside the frame. Cooper kept checking behind it, but it was only visible through the front. He shook his head, baffled.

"I don't know how people come up with stuff like that," Cooper said.

"Inspiration!" pointed out the golem from behind them.

Cooper smiled half-heartedly. "Yeah, right. Thanks."

Mateo flipped his pencil-spear in his hand and looked to Z-Blob. "Well, we better get going, right, buddy?" Z-Blob nodded. "Yeah! Izzie's waiting for us!"

He took a running jump—and leapt through the magical door, into the large, circular room on the other side. He landed and skated across the polished tile floor. It was so clean, he could see his reflection in it, green stripe in his hair and all.

"Whoa," he said.

The next thing Mateo knew, Cooper and Logan came stumbling out the door behind him. Logan landed properly, but Cooper caught his leg as he came through, and he fell into Mateo. The perfectly polished floor was slick, and Mateo went skating across the ground with Z-Blob—all the way into the nearest wall. He hit with a slam, and Logan, Cooper, and Zoey all winced. Z-Blob temporarily splattered.

"Ow," Mateo said.

"*Sluuuur,*" Z-Blob groaned.

Z-Blob pulled himself back together and bounced back onto Mateo's shoulder. Mateo finally peeled his face off the wall—and realized the brick surface was covered in tiny, perfectly circular mirrors. Had those been there before? He stepped back, scanning them where they flickered with light from the window.

"Whoa," Logan said. "Where did those come from?"

"Be at the ready." Zoey spread her legs into a stance and wobbled on the slick floor only a little. "There's another Riddle-Spoken in here, remember? Stay focused."

"I'm always focused. Like, the most focused person ever." Logan grinned at her and flipped his sunglasses on again for good measure.

"I don't think the Feathered Beast would have called you her perfect prey if that was true," Cooper said with a laugh.

The circular mirrors on the wall began to move. Mateo stepped back again, scanning them carefully as he clutched his spear. Zoey was the first person at his side, her bow already out. Cooper and Logan fell in line beside him, too, Cooper raising his hourglass and Logan his fists. But the mirrors were assembling into shapes. No, more than that. They were spelling out words.

"I . . . am . . . trapped," Mateo read the words aloud, and chills flooded down his back.

"Is this . . . still part of a riddle?" Cooper asked. He stepped forward, scanning all the perfect, clean, empty lines of the room before looking back at the mirrors. "Something seems off. The last Riddle-Spoken said that the only way the Night Hunter could have gotten to the top of the tower was if the Riddle-Spoken had gotten distracted. But what if it wasn't distracted—?"

"What if the Night Hunter trapped it?" Mateo finished his thought.

Zoey's eyes widened as the concept settled on them all. The circular mirrors began to move again, rearranging themselves to spell out a new sentence. Finally, they slowed and locked into place. Mateo read out the next message.

"He trapped me . . . in my own . . . riddle," Mateo read out to everyone. *"Release me by . . . answering it true."*

"Answering it?" Logan asked. "Wait, we've got to answer a question it's not even asking? How're we going to do that?"

Cooper rubbed his chin. "You can't answer a riddle you don't know, right? We could get it wrong. Then she'll stay trapped. And so will we. We can't get past this room without her."

"But he must have trapped her in the moving mirrors," Zoey mumbled to herself.

"So they're our best clue," Cooper agreed.

Mateo agreed, too. As Cooper, Logan, and even Zoey continued to debate, he found himself staring at his reflection, at his imperfect expression, the worry and fear battling there. The mirrors, like the floors, were polished to perfection. There wasn't a single fleck of dust, not even a smear, a fingerprint, nothing. Everything in this room, actually, was totally and completely perfect. That was why it felt so . . . cold. Unlived in. It was someone's idea of what perfect should look like.

Suddenly, it all began to make sense. Now that Mateo thought about it, the other two Riddle-Spokens had offered riddles that focused on the tools needed to dream craft. The Feathered Beast had shown them the differences between focus, a necessary principle of dream crafting, and impatience, the feeling that got in the way. The Stone Golem had revealed how fear can blind inspiration, another essential principle of dream crafting.

That meant there was only one principle left: creativity. It was the one Mateo understood the best, he'd always thought. He longed to create so much that it felt like a roaming inside him at all times. That was why he sketched so many Z-Blobs, why he wanted to create the right thing, why picking the flawless picture to submit to the art competition had been so important to him.

But looking at this room, he finally understood what the opposite of creativity was. And why.

"You know something, Cooper?" Mateo asked.

Cooper looked up from their debating. Mateo placed his hand against the nearest circular mirror. The rest of his friends quieted.

"I always thought you got everything perfect. But you said no one really gets everything right all the time, right?"

Cooper turned to face him. He looked surprised, like he'd never realized Mateo saw him that way. He smiled gently.

"Yeah, man," he said. "No one's perfect. Definitely not me. I still struggle to dream craft, but you all still care about me, right?"

Mateo nodded. "I bet the Riddle-Spoken thought this super-clean room, and these mirrors, were what 'perfect' looked like, too."

"Mateo?" Zoey asked, like she wasn't sure what he was saying.

"So you think the answer is . . . ?" Cooper walked up beside him.

The place where Mateo touched the mirror fogged up with the heat from his hand. And as he lifted it up partially, he saw the print his skin had left behind. The mirrors all shuddered together, but it sounded like they were sighing in relief.

"Perfectionism," Mateo said, "That's the answer. Perfectionism traps us and keeps us from being creative."

The mirrors all shattered.

Mateo leapt back and covered his face, blocking Z-Blob and Zoey with his body while he was at it. Zoey whipped out her cloak and helped shield Cooper and Logan. Together, they all backed away from the sea of broken glass and sharp edges of mirror.

The broken pieces didn't stay still, though. Slowly, they lifted off the ground, rising into the air in a twisting pattern, until they assembled into the sculpture of a glass woman. Her hair was filled with rainbows from the broken light, and she smiled down at them.

"You released me!" the woman said. "I was trapped in my own prison of perfection. Thank you, brave adventurers. I am the third Riddle-Spoken. I am the Glass Woman."

They all let their guard down as they looked up at the glass Riddle-Spoken. She was several feet taller than them, and she kneeled to offer her hand to Mateo. He placed his hand on hers.

"I will allow you to move on to the room above us," the Glass Woman said. "But in return, I must ask you a favor."

"A favor?" Logan asked. "I thought we just gave you one."

Cooper elbowed him.

"What? Mateo released her, right?"

Cooper elbowed him again. "Shh, man!"

But the Riddle-Spoken just smiled.

"That's right. But I believe my request is in line with what you already want. I ask you to chase away the Night Hunter from this tower. This was meant to be a safe, guarded place, where people could learn about their creative journeys and store their imaginative creations without fear of plunder. He has no place here."

She gestured to the window. "And I believe there is someone who's fought very hard to get back to you all."

Mateo turned. His heart soared—then plummeted—as he spotted Izzie outside the window, wobbling on the sill as she waved.

Chapter 12
A Daring Plan, Stan

It might have looked to the others like Izzie was once again flying by the seat of her pants, or endangering her life for a bit of fun. Yet, dangling from the window outside the third Riddle-Spoken's room at the top of a high tower was actually a result of one of Izzie's best-ever plans.

That might not have been saying much, considering how few plans Izzie made. But it was still very purposeful. And even better—the Night Hunter hadn't expected it at all.

Very few people expect someone to launch themselves out of a window, after all.

FIVE MINUTES EARLIER

Izzie was running low on dream sand in her hourglass by the time she heard noise coming from the floor beneath her.

The Night Hunter crouched on the other side of the room, fighting with the chandelier that she'd dream crafted into a giant, adorable, vicious nightmare-eating machine. It had a unicorn horn, of course. That was just for fun. But Izzie knew it wouldn't last long against the Night Hunter. Both because she was getting tired, her sand was running out, and she was having a hard time finding a way out of this situation that didn't involve her accidentally waking up—and dragging a terrible nightmare into the waking world to wreak havoc.

That was when the sound of someone slamming into a wall resonated through her feet. And she heard her brother's distant, muffled voice.

"Mateo!" she whispered.

Izzie knew she could count on her brother. She grinned to herself. She wasn't going to make him do all the work, of course. She was going to do her part this time and show him she could think of a way out of here, just like he wanted her to. And just like she wanted to. If Mateo was in here, he had to have come with their friends as well. Probably Cooper and Logan at least were nearby. Cooper would have more dream sand— she'd noticed that earlier—so if she could just get to them and warn them about the Night Hunter, they could either band together to defeat him, or run away together before he could do anyone else any more harm.

The only problem was that the Night Hunter, even fighting with the man-eating chandelier, was guarding the window. And he wasn't about to let her go.

"You think I can't ruin anything you create with fear?" the Night Hunter cried as he finally grabbed the chandelier by the unicorn horn.

"Watch me! And when you have no sand left, you'll have to tell me where Lunia is—or suffer."

He held on to the horn, and even as the chandelier fought, it began to change. Izzie clutched her Bunchu stuffie close to her chest. She couldn't let him get this last precious plushie of hers. But she had to get around him. How could she possibly do that, when he and his minions were already transforming the chandelier into a medieval mace to fight her with?

Something rolled into Izzie's foot. She turned and glanced back. All the fighting from earlier had sent a circular pillow rolling her way. It bobbed against her foot gently as the Night Hunter was busy with the chandelier turning into a mace.

Wait.

Izzie's mind sparked with an idea. She checked her hourglass one last time. She only had enough dream sand for maybe one and a half or so dream crafts. She crossed her fingers and hoped it would be enough for her new plan. She pushed away all her fears and clutched onto that distant but imperative focus she so often craved. If she could trick the Night Hunter, using his own expectations of her, she might just be able to escape on her own and meet back up with her brother and friends.

The chandelier finally and fully transformed into a diamond-studded baton in a swirl of darkness. As the Night Hunter was focused on that, Izzie quickly gripped the pillow and let it swirl with dream sand. She pictured her own Bunchu plushie as carefully as she could. And before the Night Hunter could even turn her way, she suddenly had a second Bunchu plushie in her hands. The perfect decoy.

The Night Hunter took the new diamond-studded baton in hand and whirled around. The moment he faced her, Izzie threw herself to the floor, clutching her real Bunchu out of sight, and cried out dramatically.

"No, no! What am I going to do now! Don't touch my Bunchu!" she said as she purposely left the decoy in sight.

"That's more like it!" The Night Hunter swung the baton as he came toward her. Izzie made sure the tail of her new Bunchu stuck out from her grip. "Then tell me, little dream crafter, where—is—Lunia?"

He reached down and grabbed her decoy's cotton tail. Izzie made a show of fighting for it, but he successfully ripped it out of her grasp. His small group of grimspawn cackled around him as he swung her decoy plushie over her head, taunting her.

"Lunia . . . Lunia is . . . ," Izzie started, checking that her window was open.

And it was, literally. The window that he and the grimspawn had been in front of, blocking her only exit, was finally cleared. The Night Hunter had even been relaxed enough to leave it open instead of stealing them both in here together, trapped. She grinned to herself.

"Lunia is what?" the Night Hunter demanded.

Izzie pushed herself off the ground, standing, holding Bunchu safely behind her back.

"Lunia is never going to be found by you!" she yelled.

And then sprinted past him.

"Hey!" he yelled after her. The grimspawn immediately charged for her, but Izzie was prepared. She'd noticed how slick the floor was earlier, while fighting the Night Hunter. So she leapt forward, and landed on her stomach and Bunchu. The momentum kept her soaring forward, to the window, and then all the way out of its open frame—

"Wha— What are you doing?!" the Night Hunter demanded.

Izzie twisted as she fell outside. She grinned back at him, listening for the sounds of her brother below.

"See you later, sucker!" Izzie saluted—before plummeting out the window.

And that was when she realized she hadn't thought past this part.

For a moment, Izzie was completely weightless as she tipped out into the open air, high above

the distant ground. She yelped a little as she tumbled. Wind sent her hair flying behind her, snapping at her cheeks. But she reached out her free hand. She cried out. And right when she was afraid that she might actually tumble all the way down and slam into the ground below—

Her hand snagged on a window frame, and she slammed into a sheet of glass.

It didn't break, though her face basically flattened against the surface. It hurt a bit, but not nearly as bad as falling several stories would have, so Izzie was just relieved. But through the window, she spotted something that made everything better.

Mateo, Cooper, Logan, and Zoey were all inside the room below, just like she'd thought. She beamed. Her plan worked! She had escaped the Night Hunter and now she was back with her team!

Well, almost. She'd work on getting the kinks out of her plans in the future. For now, she was just happy to see Mateo's head turning her way.

"Mateo!" she called. She waved Bunchu at him, then nearly tipped backward. Mateo let out a muffled cry, and he ran over to her.

"Izzie!" he said. She could barely hear him through the glass. "What're you doing out there? Where's the Night Hunter?"

"Not far behind me probably, so if you could let me in there, that would be great!" She grinned.

A giant glass woman shuffled into place behind Mateo. Izzie's eyes widened as she took in her prismatic hair, glowing hands, and gentle smile. She was—so—cool! What kind of awesome adventure had Izzie just missed?

Fortunately, the glass woman opened the window for her, and Izzie tipped herself inside. Mateo caught her as she stumbled. Z-Blob greeted her with a cheerful gurgle.

"I missed you, too, green guy!" Izzie said back. She beamed at her brother next. "Mateo, I'm so glad to see you!"

"Izzie, I'm so glad you're okay!" Mateo wrapped her in a hug. "I'm sorry I got so mad at you. How'd you escape?" He pulled back and shook his head. "No, you know what? We need to get out of here."

"Waaaay ahead of you," Logan said. He was across the room, and he had his hand on the doorknob of the floating door. "Let's leave, man. Lunia's not even here."

"She's not?" Izzie asked.

"Long story," Zoey said.

"Oh, wait, Zoey!" Izzie said. She beamed at her. "You came after all! I knew you would."

Zoey shrugged. "Whatever." But there was a slight smile in the corner of her mouth.

Suddenly, the ceiling above them shuddered. Dust fell like rain from the rafters. The Glass Woman lifted her head.

"Flee, young ones," she said. "The Night Hunter is coming for you. And if you can't give him Lunia's location, you'll pay in far worse ways."

Chapter 13

Dream Siblings

It was mere moments after the glass Riddle-Spoken had warned them that the Night Hunter, with his pack of grimspawn, had broken through the ceiling.

The floor erupted above their heads and fell in large chunks of wood, smearing the perfectly polished tiles with dust, dirt, and junk from above. The Night Hunter landed in the middle of them—Izzie and Mateo on one side, the glass Riddle-Spoken, Zoey, Logan, and Cooper on the other.

The Night Hunter snapped his fingers, and the wave of grimspawn hissed their sharp, glowing teeth at the others. Zoey whipped out her bow and flung arrows. But the grimspawn charged them relentlessly.

"Leave them alone!" Mateo called out. He spun his pencil-spear and ran forward. He swiped one of the grimspawn and sent it tumbling, but the others were too fast and too determined. They crowded in around Zoey and the others, pushing them back toward the door.

"You brought the Riddle-Spoken back, I see," the Night Hunter said. "Well, I guess I should have just corrupted her and all the Riddle-Spokens earlier. I'll do that now, then."

He readied himself to destroy her.

"No!" Zoey yelled. "I'm not letting you steal other people's imaginations again!"

Behind her, Cooper had managed to scramble to the floating door they'd come through. He thrust it open and directed the others away.

"Quickly!" he said. "Run!"

Zoey fought off the grimspawn to give the Riddle-Spoken, Logan, and Cooper time to get through the door. The boys rushed the Glass Woman back in the direction they'd come. Mateo briefly heard the golem receive them as he tried to bat grimspawn off Zoey, and Izzie kicked her way through them. But the nightmares pushed too hard, and Zoey tumbled backward through the door.

"Mateo!" she called.

The Night Hunter leapt forward, slammed the door shut, and suddenly sliced it in half. The door fell as two useless planks on the floor, joining the scraps of ceiling and rafters. Mateo panted, lifting his pencil-spear. Izzie raised her fists, clutching Bunchu to her chest. They were trapped here now with the Night Hunter. Mateo glanced around, assessing their chances, the situation. How likely they were to get out.

They were both low on dream sand. Both sweaty and with few weapons and options. Z-Blob hunched himself, looking ready to fight, but with so little dream sand, what was Mateo going to turn him into? Plus, they had a bunch of debris they'd have to fight through, and the grimspawn that hadn't followed Zoey and the others through the door were still here, gathered around the Night Hunter's feet.

"It's not looking good," Mateo whispered.

Izzie squeezed his hand. "We can do it, Broseph."

And despite everything—Mateo believed that, too. Even if everything was stacked against them.

Mateo pointed his spear at the Night Hunter. "Let's go, Night Hunter!"

The Night Hunter scanned him and Izzie, and Z-Blob and the Bunchu plushie, up and down. Before busting up laughing.

"You think I'm scared of *you?*" the Night Hunter asked, practically guffawing. "I have no idea where this unreasonable confidence suddenly came from, but it's hilarious. I mean, look at you two! You might be full of powerful imagination, but what does it matter if you can't focus long enough to turn it into anything?" He pointed at Izzie. "And you"—he addressed Mateo—"are too scared of not getting everything perfectly right to make *anything* unless your life basically depends on it. Just tell me where Lunia is, children." He clenched his claws menacingly. "You're not going to defeat the Nightmare King by the end of all of this anyway. Make it easier on yourself. What do you say, kid?"

Mateo considered telling him the truth: that the rumors about Lunia were a wild-goose chase. But he knew the Night Hunter wouldn't give up fighting them just for that. And if the rumors could keep the Nightmare King's forces busy while they continued training, even for another night, it would be worth the secret.

"Don't talk to my brother that way! He's a creative genius!" Izzie yelled. "He's super talented, and just because he overthinks sometimes and isn't ready to show everyone his work yet"—she reached and grabbed his hand—"doesn't mean he won't one day, or that his work isn't awesome!"

"Yeah!" Mateo grabbed her hand back. Their hourglasses clinked together, and their depleted sand began to glow gold within their enclosures. "And just because Izzie doesn't always focus doesn't mean her fearlessness and imagination aren't totally inspiring! She's full of sunshine. And you know what Nightmares fear?"

Their hourglasses glowed brighter. Mateo could feel it even before he could see it. His mind tingled, and his heart began to pound with a flying, free feeling that felt like dream crafting— only even better. Izzie's eyes shone with the light, and she turned a confident grin onto the widening, worried eyes of the Night Hunter.

"Nightmares fear the light!" Izzie finished.

The light encompassed them and their hourglasses like a brilliant sun.

All at once, Mateo could feel himself dream crafting. Only, it wasn't just him doing it. He could feel Izzie's imagination and his swirling together in the light in front of them, filled with her unicorns, and Bunchu, and his Z-Blob, and sci-fi fun. The elements began to draw together. And even though Mateo had no idea how it was happening, he embraced it.

It was like sewing together pure creativity. All the fear Mateo had about getting things right loosened up and, for a moment, faded. Izzie's fearlessness threaded through him. Where Izzie wasn't the best about thinking things through, Mateo's careful, stable imagination stepped in and steadied it. It was wordless, pure creation: and without even speaking to each other, Mateo and Izzie knew what they needed to make.

Their imagination elements collected and transformed with their dream sand before their eyes. The Night Hunter stumbled back as the light grew blinding. Mechanical whirring and bright colors filled the air, and out from the light leapt their new dream-crafted creation—

A sci-fi fantasy monster unlike either world had ever seen.

A giant bunny-cyborg hybrid, with razor metal claws on its fluffy paws, and Z-Blob in a suite of armor, dotted with gauges and a drone arm attachment, rose out of the dust and light.

Mateo usually liked to make cool things like jets, drones, helicopters, or cyborgs. But this time, he could see his ideas had merged with Izzie's love of fantasy and action. And their ideas were like peanut butter and jelly. Like chocolate and strawberry. Like—

Well, like Mateo and Izzie.

"You're amazing!" Izzie exclaimed, staring at their beautiful monster.

"Get 'im, Bunchu Z-Bot!" Mateo pointed at the Night Hunter.

"Bunchu Z-Bot?" Izzie grinned at him.

He shrugged with a confident smile. "The name just came to me."

The Night Hunter's eyes widened as their mechanical Bunchu twisted around, baring its metal teeth at him. Z-Blob, seated at the helm of the creature, gurgled threateningly as well.

Bunchu Z-Bot narrowed its rainbow eyes on him, twisting its ears back, and growled.

"Hey, wait, let's negotiate here . . ." The Night Hunter backed away, looking for something to grab, some means of escape. "You know the Nightmare King will just send more recruits. It won't stop here!"

"Get him!" Mateo and Izzie cried.

Bunchu Z-Bot leapt on the Night Hunter, its jaws wide. He leapt right and avoided the first bite. But the metal jaws chomped his way, never letting up for a second. He ran across the tower and rolled to the window. Bunchu's metal claws slammed the ground in front of him. The Night Hunter jumped into the window and broke it.

"You haven't seen the last of me!" he cried as the glass shattered. "The Nightmare King won't be stopped, even if you can dream bash. No one, not even the rumor of Lunia, can stop him—"

Bunchu whipped around, swinging his cotton ball-and-chain tail. The end slapped the Night Hunter in the face. He wobbled his arms, trying

to catch his balance—and then tumbled out the window for good.

"Aaaaagh!" His scream faded.

Izzie and Mateo ran to the window. Far below, grimspawn caught him before he could hit the ground. The Night Hunter tottered as they carted him away, into the horizon. He adjusted his hat and pointed back up at them.

"We'll get you, dream chasers!" he yelled as the grimspawn turned out of sight. "One of these days, your imagination will run dry, and when you can't stack up against our criticism, you'll be fuel for nightmares!"

They watched the nightmare leagues vanish beyond. Izzie blew a raspberry.

"Sore loser much?" She snorted.

Mateo laughed. "Yeah. Whenever they come back, we'll always be there to help protect dreamers."

"That's right, we will!"

The floor rocked, and Mateo and Izzie stumbled as Bunchu Z-Bot ran up to them. It knelt on its claws, wiggling its tail, and blinked up at them with its rainbow eyes. Z-Bot gurgled from the creature's armor.

"Wow!" Mateo looked their dream-crafted creature over. "Thanks, Bunchu Z-Bot! I can't believe we really made you together!"

"I can!" Izzie said. "Because Bunchu and Z-Blob look even more *awesome* than usual!"

The girl bounced on her toes.

"Look at you!" She grabbed the giant's face. "Who's the cutest? You! That's right, it's you, my little bunny!"

Bunchu Z-Bot's ball-and-chain tail wiggled harder. Izzie continued to baby-talk to it.

Mateo laughed. "Yeah, it is pretty awesome." He stroked the beast's snout and smiled, slowly, over at his sister. "We're pretty awesome, Izzie."

Her eyes sparkled as she looked at him. "So . . . we're cool, Bro-seph?"

"Always," Mateo said.

They hugged. And after a long, warm moment, Izzie peeked over his shoulder.

"Um. So how do we get down from here, anyway?" She pointed back at the broken door left behind by the Night Hunter. "That's how you got up here, right?"

"Good question," Mateo said.

They both looked at Bunchu Z-Bot. Bunchu Z-Bot straightened up at the attention. Z-Blob, seated in the armor, gurgled. Bunchu's nose wiggled, and together, they shook until a click sounded in the room, and helicopter blades began to fold out of the creature's metallic sides. Mateo grinned.

He looked over at his sister. "I think I've got an idea. Why don't we take a page out of your book?"

Izzie squealed with delight.

Chapter 14

Team Tower

Zoey, Cooper, and Logan had their hands full with the grimspawn in the golem Riddle-Spoken's room. Zoey whipped out her bow and kept sending arrows flying at the greedy, frightening creatures. One spiraled in midair—and bounced off the Stone Golem's head.

"Ow," the golem said. He put his rocky hands on his hips and scanned Zoey, Cooper, and Logan before his flame eyes landed on the glass Riddle-Spoken. "What's all this mess you've brought to my room?"

A grimspawn leapt, biting, for Cooper's leg. Zoey slid across the floor, and slapped her weapon across its head so it hissed as it flipped upside down and landed on its skull.

"We're a bit busy!" Zoey gritted her teeth. "And Mateo and Izzie are trapped in the glass Riddle-Spoken's room with the Night Hunter!"

"That sounds serious," the golem tapped his chin. "Fearful, even."

A grimspawn leapt on Zoey's cloak and started to gnaw on it, inching toward her neck. Cooper leapt forward and kicked it off, looking nervous but determined.

"You're telling us!" he said.

The glass Riddle-Spoken turned to the golem. "Friend! We must help them get rid of these nightmares before they overrun the tower!"

"The Feathered Beast would love to help with that," said the Stone Golem. "Would you like me to go get her?"

For being a guardian of fear, he was very, unfortunately, polite.

"Just do something!" Zoey called out. She span around and flung arrows into three grimspawn before they could dog-pile her. "Anything! Before they take us down!"

She was getting annoyed—working with other people wasn't her strong suit anymore, and now she was trying to work with several. She was almost mad that she'd decided to come along after all. But she wouldn't have forgiven herself if Mateo, Izzie, Cooper, or Logan got hurt because of her, either.

Zoey would never admit it out loud—but they were important to her.

"Hey, big dude!" Logan called up to the golem. He jumped on his stone foot, and the golem blinked down at him. Logan put his sunglasses on again. "Mind turning the lights up?"

"Oh!" The golem straightened. "That's right! Everyone close your eyes, then."

Zoey got one more hit on the grimspawn before swishing her cloak around her and Cooper. "Close your eyes!" she yelled.

The Stone Golem's lantern brightened. "Here we go!"

The flash of his light was so brilliant, so burning and stunning, that Zoey could feel it even through the fabric of her cloak. All around them, the grimspawn shrieked as the light devoured them. Suddenly, everything went silent. Zoey dropped her cape to find herself alone with only Cooper, Logan, and the two Riddle-Spokens left in the room. She sighed in relief.

"Logan! That was so smart!" Cooper ran over and clapped his shoulder.

"Well, you know. Sometimes I can focus, too." Logan shrugged, smiling hesitantly at first, like he was genuinely touched by the compliment. But then he cleared his throat and turned a wink and a grin on Zoey. "What'd you think, Zoey? Pretty good, right?"

She was annoyed about a lot of things. But she had to give it to him—it *was* smart. So she sighed, striding past him, and nodded. "Sure, Logan. Nice job."

He perked up even more and followed her across the room. The golem scratched his lantern head, and the glass Riddle-Spoken gestured them to the blue door.

"If you ask, the Feathered Beast will send you through the fast exit so you can leave the tower quickly," the glass Riddle-Spoken said. "Since the Night Hunter destroyed the door, it's your best option to get back to your friends safely."

"Then let's go," Zoey said.

She led them through the door, intent on checking that the rest of her friends—she'd never call them that out loud, but they were definitely friends in her heart—were all right.

Just as Zoey, Logan, and Cooper exited the tower at the ground floor, Mateo and Izzie landed a short distance away on a giant bunny-and-Z-Blob-cyborg creation.

"Whoa!" Logan jumped back. "Is that— Mateo and Izzie? They got down pretty fast!"

Zoey folded her arms and smirked. But it was softer than usual. Almost a smile. "Huh. Looks like the sibling dream team is back together. They must have defeated the Night Hunter."

Cooper noticed Zoey's eyes soften. He smiled a little. "Sounds like you're happy about that. Got a soft spot for them, huh?"

Instantly, she scowled. "Whatever. It was just—uh—annoying having them fight. That's all. Can't get anything done when they're squabbling."

Cooper could tell she was lying. But Logan threw his arm over her, laughing. "I know, right?" he said. "I can't believe I'm saying this, but I can't wait to hear Izzie talk about her dumb anime stuff again. It's way better than their sulking."

Zoey pushed his arm off, but before any of them could say anything, Mr. Oz and Albert called out to them. They turned, and Mr. Oz sighed in relief.

"I was so worried about you all! Was that Izzie out the window I saw earlier?" He shook his head and lowered his laser cannon. "It's the strangest thing! All the grimspawn have up and left, along with the Night Hunter. Not sure why, but I say we make the most of it and resume our search for Lunia."

"About that," Zoey started.

She didn't get to finish, since Mateo and Izzie leapt off their metal Bunchu monster and ran toward them. Mateo and Izzie waved and called their names.

"Everyone! Everyone! Meet Bunchu Z-Bot!" Izzie landed in front of them along with the big furry creature. Immediately, she snuggled its soft nose. Bunchu Z-Bot made a growling, gurgling sound that made it clear how much it loved cuddles. "Isn't she *beautiful?* Mateo and I made her together!"

Zoey raised an eyebrow. "Together? Like— you came up with the idea, and Mateo made it?"

"No!" Mateo strode out confidently to stand next to Izzie. "We combined our dream sand, since we were both low and, like, dream-bashed Bunchu Z-Bot together!"

Cooper blinked. "Huh. How exactly did that work?"

"No idea. It's hard to explain," Izzie said. "But it was awesome!"

Cooper smiled. "Well, I'm just glad you two seem back to normal."

Izzie and Mateo looked at each other. Mateo nodded.

"Yeah," he said. "We are. Better than normal, actually."

"Excellent. Now that we've got this handled, we have just enough time to look for those Lunia rumors," Mr. Oz said. He gestured to everyone and started scanning the square. "Strap up, everyone. We've got to find any trace of her if we can!"

Mateo, Zoey, Logan, and Cooper all looked at each other. Logan shrugged.

"Yeah, uh, bad news, Mr. Oz," he said.

"She's not even nearby," Zoey said, rough and sharp. "One of the Riddle-Spokens in there was just throwing out some of her old stuff, so that must have been where the rumors came from."

"That's such a disappointment," Mr. Oz said, shaking his head. He sighed, clearly deflated, and rubbed his forehead. "Oy. I can't believe we wasted so much time."

"I wouldn't call it a waste," Mateo said. "I learned a lot today about dream crafting."

"Me too," Izzie said. "And that means we'll be even more powerful the next time we have to face the Night Hunter or even the Nightmare King!" She punched at the air. "They better watch out! The dream chasers aren't to be messed with!"

Mr. Oz and Albert looked at each other, then turned smiles on the group.

"Sounds like today's excursion at least helped you develop your dream crafting principles then," Albert said. "That's essential to being a good dream chaser and eventually defeating the Nightmare King."

"He's right," Mr. Oz agreed. "Everyone's creative journey is different, but we're all growing and learning. I'm glad to hear you've all seen that in practice today."

"And I'm glad we can get out of here now." Albert thumbed back to the distant Fantasy Gates, back where they'd parked the jet. "I don't want to run into any more nightmares tonight. Let them search for baseless rumors while we go get some much-needed relaxation time."

Everyone agreed with a light laugh, and Albert and Mr. Oz led the group back down the path in the direction they'd come from. Mateo, Cooper, and Logan eagerly filled Izzie in on all the incredible Riddle-Spokens they'd met on their way up to her, and Izzie oohed and aahed at the vivid descriptions of them.

"I wish I'd met them!" Izzie said. "They sound so huggable!"

Mateo just laughed. That was the most Izzie reaction he could possibly think of. Soon enough, they arrived back at the jet. Mrs. Castillo was still there in her turtle caravan. It had moved a little bit since they had left, but not far. She waved to them as they headed back up the jet's ramp together.

"Look at you, talented chicos!" Mrs. Castillo called. "Did you find what you were searching for?"

"Um, yes and no, Mrs. Castillo," Mateo said. "Thanks for your help earlier."

"Of course, mijo!" She beamed at them and patted her turtle's counter. "Always here for you if you need. But it seems to me perhaps you found what you most needed, even if it wasn't what you thought you were looking for?"

Mateo paused in the doorway as the others filed in past him. Izzie smiled as she walked by. He clutched his pencil and looked down at Z-Blob, where he was jumping his way into the jet. Mrs. Castillo had a great point. Maybe what you want isn't always what you need. And what Mateo *really* needed in the waking world? What he needed to do with the art competition? He had a much better idea of what that looked like now.

"Gracias, Mrs. Castillo!" he called. "We'll see you tomorrow night."

"See you then, mijo!"

Mateo stepped inside, and the jet packed up to leave. Outside the window, Mateo watched Zoey mount Zian instead. She never went back with them in the jet. But she waved. She'd probably meet them back at the landing. Mateo smiled.

Mateo and Izzie sat together as Izzie regaled Cooper and Logan with the full dream-crafting, bashing event that led to their magical creation. Izzie tried really hard to look bored, but a smile hovered around the corner of her mouth and betrayed how happy she secretly was. Cooper and Mateo glanced at each other across the aisle, and Cooper winked. Mateo nodded. It was good to have a sibling who supported him. And he'd make sure to support her, too. Even if they still probably needed to talk about respecting each other's pacing.

"I was right," Logan said as he lounged back in his seat—without a belt still. "It is weirdly nice to hear all that chatter again. Heh." He adjusted his hat. Paused for a few second. Then sighed.

"Nope, it's old again. Izzie! Can you, like, *breathe* between words?"

"Never!" she cackled.

Mr. Oz and Albert laughed in the front seat as they zoomed off back to the dream landing.

Chapter 15

Home Again

When Mateo woke up, Izzie was hovering over him in her pajamas.

"Thanks for saving me, bro," she said.

He smiled. "No problem, Izzie," he said. He sat up in bed. Z-Blob was waiting for him, too, perched on his nightstand. All three of them looked over at his desk. It was still covered in sketches—none of which felt right to him, especially since he'd made them when he was stressed out and afraid. Mateo sighed a little, and Izzie grimaced.

"What're you going to do?" she asked. "If you want, I can tell Mr. G that I signed you up for the competition. I'm sure he'll pull you out! I was trying to be supportive, but I shouldn't have pushed you into something you weren't ready for," Izzie admitted, fidgeting with her hands. "You're always patient with me when I can't focus. You don't expect that I'll just wake up one day and be different. So I shouldn't have done that to you, either. I know I said it earlier, but—I really am sorry I tried to rush you, Mateo."

"Thanks, Izzie." Mateo got up and squeezed Izzie in a tight hug. "I forgive you. And honestly, you were right. I have to learn not to be so scared of what other people think of what I make. If I keep waiting for something I make to be perfect, I'll never share. Or I may stop drawing completely. I'd really hate it if that happened."

"So would I," Izzie agreed.

After a moment, they separated. Mateo looked over at his desk and all his scribbles. Z-Blob bounced over to the desk, leapt onto the far right corner, and burbled encouragingly. A flash of bravery flooded through Mateo.

"It's time to get to work, if I'm going to enter that art show today," Mateo said.

Izzie gasped in delight. Mateo crossed the room with new, brimming confidence and picked up his pencil, an image already forming in his mind. This wasn't quite dream crafting. But the waking world had its own sort of magic.

"Yes, Mateo!" Izzie whisper-cheered. "You got this! Go, bro, go!"

Mateo sat down, pencil ready, and got to work. Sure, he was still scared. Nervous. Kind of felt like puking, even. But he focused and let himself be more excited about expressing himself, about creating from inspiration, than about what Mr. Guerrero and the judges would think about how good his work was. Maybe no one would see his work and think he was a great artist. Maybe someone would judge him and criticize his skills. But he didn't want to get stuck in the Glass Woman's trap. And he wanted to believe in himself, in his work, in what he could do, the same way Izzie believed in him.

Mateo let himself draw and sketch and erase and shade without letting the fear drag him down. When he was done, Mateo sat back and looked at his work. He waited. And he felt satisfaction and surety sweep up his chest like a warm summer day in New York City. Mateo smiled. That was it. It was ready.

"Hey, Izzie," he called her over. "Come look!"

She'd waited respectfully this time, no peeking or prodding. And when he called her name, she jumped up from her bed, beaming, and came to look over his shoulder. She took one long look at it, taking in the sweeping lines, before squealing.

"This looks amazing, Mateo!" she said. "Mr. Guerrero is going to love it. But more important"—she looked at him—"do you like it?"

He grinned up at her. "I love it!"

Maybe the drawing wasn't perfect. He'd only done it this morning, after all. But he wasn't trying to make it perfect this time. This time, he just wanted it to feel right. And it finally did. That finally felt more important than anyone else's opinion.

He was ready to show it to the world. He wasn't scared anymore. Or at least, he wasn't going to let his fear hold him back this time. Today, Mateo was going to be brave.

"Let's get ready for school, Izzie!" Mateo carefully took the drawing in hand. "I have an art competition to enter."

Chapter 16
The Art Show

Izzie and Mateo stood in front of the art room at their school. Mateo's heart pounded in his chest as he scanned the closed classroom door and Mr. Guerrero's colorful ART-STRAVAGANZA flyers. He'd barely submitted the piece on time the day he'd declared he would so confidently. It was Friday now, a week later, and he was finally going to see his artwork on display. The rest of the classes would be released soon to come and stare at his work. He was going to have a piece out in the world. And find out what people thought of his work. The judging eyes of a bunch of strangers weighing the value of his work.

Mateo had felt pretty brave the day he submitted his drawing. But today, his courage deserted him. He was extremely, gut-flippingly, hide-himself-in-a-locker anxious. But he kept himself cool on the outside as he remembered everything that had brought him to this moment. He hadn't beaten all those Riddle-Spokens for nothing. And after all, he'd already submitted the drawing. There was no going back now.

"Are you nervous?" Izzie asked Mateo.

Strangely enough, Mateo didn't want to go back. He wanted to see this through, nervous or not.

"Yeah," he answered. "I'm still scared. But I know I made what I wanted to make. So let's go in and face the music."

"Or more like the art!" Izzie said brightly.

Mateo laughed a little. "Yeah. Let's go in and face the art." He looked back at his backpack. "What do you say, Z-Blob?"

Z-Blob stuck his gooey green head out of Mateo's unzipped backpack. *"Slurrpp!"*

Mateo and Izzie laughed. They were about to step forward when a voice called out from down the hallway.

"Did you really think we were going to let you go in alone?"

Mateo turned and found Cooper and Logan there, striding down the hall toward them. Logan was wearing the same sunglasses he'd brought into the dream world, like he was trying to make sure nobody forgot he was the cool one, even if he was about to walk into an art show early. Cooper was smiling, even if he had slight shadows under his eyes from all the homework he must have binged through to be here.

"You made it!" Izzie jumped excitedly. "I'm so glad. You managed to get out of class early, Cooper?"

He rubbed the back of his head as he stopped in front of them. "Yeah. My parents wouldn't like to hear about me leaving class early, but I told the teacher I was friends with one of the artists!"

"And of course *I* came," Logan said, grinning and folding his arms proudly. "I'm not going to miss a chance to laugh at Matty."

"It's Mateo," Mateo grumbled.

Cooper elbowed Logan in the side. Logan coughed, and Cooper smiled at Mateo.

"We couldn't miss a chance to support you," Cooper said. "I know what it's like when no one has the time for that."

Mateo smiled as he looked from Cooper to Logan to his sister. The nervousness still coiled in his stomach, but it was a bit easier to handle knowing he had friends at his side.

"All right!" he said, and turned to the classroom door. "Then no more stalling. Let's face the art!"

They stepped inside to find the art room transformed. Where Mr. Guerrero usually had it set up with long tables covered in paint, pencils, and papers, all the tables had been folded away, and all the walls had been turned into a stunning art gallery. Colors and imagination decorated the walls on sheets of paper, divided into section based on the medium used: graphite, pastels, watercolor paint, acrylic paint, pen-and-ink. There were even a few submitted sculptures on Mr. Guerrero's desk.

Mr. Guerrero spotted them from behind his desk and waved. Mateo hadn't seen him since he'd turned in his submission. He smiled sheepishly and waved back.

"Come on in!" Mr. Guerrero called, and gestured them toward the rest of the room.

There were a few students and a couple parents milling around the area. Mateo took a deep breath and led the way over to his section: graphite. People parted, and he spotted someone standing in front of his drawing.

It was Zoey.

Mateo's mouth opened in surprise. He'd invited her to the show earlier this week—well, kind of. He'd stumbled over himself for most of it but managed to get out the time and day at least. She'd just nodded, so Mateo hadn't thought she'd actually come. But there she was, in her dark clothes with her hood up, staring at Mateo's drawing where it hung on the wall.

Mateo's heart fluttered as she examined the picture thoughtfully. He'd drawn a big picture of Z-Blob, inspired by his and Izzie's dream craft creation. It wasn't Bunchu Z-Bot, of course. But it mixed sci-fi and fantasy elements, so Z-Blob, as a cyborg, had a magic staff and wore sweeping wizard robes. Was she analyzing the way he'd blended the two genres together? Did she think the flags he'd added in the background were silly? He wasn't sure whether her highly focused attention made him feel even more nervous—or flattered. But his cheeks flushed warm either way.

Zoey turned as they came up behind her. "Cool stuff, Mateo." She nodded back at the drawing.

His heart turned as gooey as Z-Blob. She thought it was cool?

"Thanks, Zoey," he said.

She nodded. "It's really creative, even if . . ."

"It didn't win," Izzie whispered.

Mateo followed Izzie's gaze to the frame around his picture. Oh. The first, second, and third place winners all had ribbons on theirs. So it was true. He hadn't won after all. People had judged his work, and they didn't think it was worth a prize.

Mateo's heart crumpled. Z-Blob poked his head out of his backpack and leaned against him, like he was trying to comfort him. Izzie bit her bottom lip. He nearly expected her to tell him to stay positive, but she didn't. This time, she just looped her arm through his and squeezed his arm in a hug.

"I'm sorry, Mateo," she whispered. "For what it's worth, I think it's great."

He'd thought it was great, too. But the fact remained that he hadn't won. After all that work, after all the courage it had taken to enter— Mateo's work still wasn't good enough. Just like those kids had said all those years ago.

For a moment, he could barely look at his friends. They'd all come to cheer him on, and he'd still failed. He should have just waited for next year after all. Why wasn't he better at his work already? Shame welled up inside him.

"Mateo?"

All five of them jumped as Mr. Guerrero came up behind them. Mateo met Mr. Guerrero's kind eyes, and even though the teacher smiled, Mateo still felt embarrassed to think his work hadn't lived up to Mr. Guerrero's hopes.

"I know you didn't win this year. You must be disappointed," Mr. Guerrero said as he smiled down at Mateo and handed him a sheet of paper. "But winning isn't everything. Every entry gets feedback on their piece," he said. Mateo took the page carefully. "You did something very difficult this year, overcoming fear. So I hope you'll be patient with yourself and continue to grow as an artist. Thanks for submitting your work, Mateo. I was really happy to see it. And I hope I get to see it next year, too."

The words were like a warm, comforting blanket around Mateo's heart. It was still hard for him to smile, but he tried. He'd half expected Mr. Guerrero to look disappointed in him for not creating something better. But he could tell the teacher had meant every word he'd said.

"Thanks, Mr. Guerrero." He clutched the paper.

"What's it say?" Izzie craned her head over his shoulder.

Zoey, Cooper, and Logan all huddled in around him. Together, they read the message. And Mateo's heart warmed even more with the words written there.

Mateo,

You've done a lot of great work here. The mash-up of fantasy and science fiction elements in your character are imaginative, extremely fun, and creative. You also have great sense of movement and a memorable, expressive character. You could do with some work on your value scale and shading techniques, but this is an amazing beginning to your journey as an artist. Remember that you don't need to master everything at once. Patience is key to being an artist. Keep creating, and keep sharing. The world needs an imagination like yours!

Mr. G—

Mateo's aching heart slowly melted. That was right. Patience. The boy understood that he needed to be a bit more patient with himself, like the Feathered Beast had said. If he was patient, then he wouldn't feel as liable to get trapped in perfectionism, like the Glass Woman, or blinded by fear, like his experience with the Stone Golem.

Mateo might not have won today, but he could still be a great artist. Mr. Guerrero himself said he already had done a lot of great work here. Mateo just needed to give himself time to grow.

Cooper patted Mateo's shoulder as he looked at the paper. "Yeah," he said. "He's right. The world does need work like yours."

"The waking world," Zoey added, "As much as the dream world."

"Well, I think the judges are obviously really dumb," Logan said, way too loud, and everyone looked their way. "Z-Blob is super awesome in your drawing! Even *I* can't laugh at him. He should've at least won first place. The art teacher must have something in both of his eyes."

Z-Blob stuck his out his backpack and gurgled, as if thanking him for the compliment. For some reason, that was all it took to break Mateo's tension, and he started to laugh. Logan looked surprised before he started grinning. Izzie started laughing, too, and before long, they were all chuckling.

"Thanks, Logan," Mateo said. He looked to Z-Blob. "You do look pretty great, huh?"

Z-Blob made a charmed, bubbling sound.

The laughter settled down a bit, and Izzie smiled up at Mateo sincerely.

"You know, today might not have gone as planned"—Izzie hugged Mateo's arm—"but I'm still proud of you, Bro-seph."

Mateo grinned, surrounded by his friends.

He'd been judged by strangers, and he hadn't even gotten an honorable mention, let alone a first-place ribbon. But for some reason, he felt like he'd won today. Sure, he hadn't won the art show. But he'd won in his first step sharing his work. He'd won in the battle against his own perfectionism, fear, and impatience—just like he and his friends had solved the Riddle-Spokens' challenges. Just like he and Izzie had won against the Night Hunter.

Mateo let his creativity finally be free, and that meant he was really on his way to being a great artist.

And you know what?

That was triumph enough for him.

Epilogue

While Izzie, Cooper, Zoey, and Logan celebrated Matteo's debut in the school art competition, the Night Hunter had no reason to be happy. After all, he had been summoned to the Shadowkeep, the Nightmare King's eerie fortress, right after he returned to the Grim Realm.

As the Night Hunter entered the gloomy chamber, he saw his master waiting for him on his throne, set on a huge boulder by the opposite wall. Crowds of curious grimspawn scurried around the dark room. The Nightmare King sat motionless except to shoot an icy look at the Night Hunter.

"I heard you failed to stop the dream chasers," hissed the evil ruler of the Grim Realm. "And you got thrown out the tower's window."

"He got thrown out the window! He got thrown out the window!" the wicked grimspawn cackled.

"Silence!" the Nightmare King told them. "Let's hear it from the Night Hunter. Let him explain how this scandalous turn of events was even possible."

The Night Hunter only stared at the floor. "Your Darkness," he started. "I apologize. I know I let you down again, but the failure was pure accident. The dream chasers were just . . . lucky. I am confident that their good fortune will soon come to an end. Give me another chance, and I will not fail you."

The Nightmare King stood up and climbed down his elevated throne to stand level with his second-in-command. He looked straight into the Night Hunter's eyes.

"I am running out of patience," he said in almost a whisper. "I don't know yet if I want to give you another chance or take matters into my own hands. I'm almost as terrifying as I was years ago, so a bunch of kids shouldn't be a challenge for me. One thing is certain: we cannot waste more time! I can't let the dream chasers find Lunia before me!"

The Nightmare King was now shouting so loudly the walls trembled.

"Excuse me, Your Darkness," one of the grimspawn offered. "But didn't you once say that even Lunia could not stop you from turning the dream world into a realm of nightmares?"

The Nightmare King shot a furious look at the creature.

"Get out of here!" he yelled. "All of you! Out! I need to think!"

The grimspawn cringed and rushed out the door. The Night Hunter followed them, but when he was in the doorway, he turned to look back. The Nightmare King sat on his throne again, staring blankly ahead.

I wouldn't want to be in the dream chasers' shoes if he decides to go after them, the Night Hunter thought as he closed the door behind him. *He's much more terrifying now than he was years ago. . . .*

Glossary

Albert

In the waking world, he is a figurine on Mr. Oswald's desk, but in the dream world, he is his close friend. This fast-talking Texan chimpanzee is the more logical of the two and does his best to stop Mr. Oswald from being too reckless.

Aware dreamer

This is someone who realizes that the dream world is real, can participate in others' dreams, and when awake, remembers everything.

Bunchu

Bunchu is Izzie's precious plushie rabbit that comes from her favorite anime. It's cute as can be but can become a huge beast in the dream world, too.

Bunchu Z-Bot

A dream-crafted combination of the beloved Bunchu and loyal Z-Blob, Bunchu Z-Bot is a force to be reckoned with, and cute, to boot.

Cooper

He is Mateo's old friend who loves sports, cars, and technology. He's great at everything he tries to do, but he has to work harder than the other dream crafters to get his dream crafts right.

Dream chaser

This is an aware dreamer who has been recruited to the Night Bureau and trained in dream crafting to protect the dream world from the nightmare forces and save captive dreamers.

Dream crafter

This is one who participates in the dreams of others and has dream-crafting skills (the ability to create or change objects within the dream world). Everything a dream crafter creates is called dream craft. A successful dream craft requires creativity, inspiration, and focus.

Dream landing

This is a place where aware dreamers appear when they arrive in the dream world. In the dream landing there are numerous doors that lead to different dream realms.

Dream realms

These amazing islands make up the dream world. The dream realms are populated by the creatures from dreams of sleeping people. There are many realms in the dream world; for example: the Fantasy Realm, the Cyber Realm, the Double Realm, the Candy Realm, and the Nightmare King's Grim Realm.

Dream sand

This is the sand inside the hourglasses used by dream chasers. It helps create more stable and long-lasting dream crafts. If a dream crafter uses all the sand in their hourglass, they won't be able to create new dream crafts until the next time they visit the dream world.

Dream world

This is a vast, fantastical world of dreams and imagination where every sleeping person travels to every night without knowing it. This extraordinary place consists of many wildly different realms, each existing as an island floating in the sky. Aware dreamers can travel between all realms at will.

Feathered Beast

This is the first Riddle-Spoken that guards the legendary beasts' tower. This giant serpent with metal feathers tests trespassers on the first principle of dream crafting.

Glass Woman

The third and last Riddle-Spoken is a tall woman made of glass. She tests trespassers on their understanding of perfectionism and how it can get in the way of creativity.

Grimspawn

The Nightmare King's low-level minions are devious if small, and together, they create quite the army on a mission to snuff out dreams. They are created from the imaginations of the dreaming kids the Nightmare King captures and can take forms and personalities inspired by the imaginations of the kids they came from.

Izzie

Mateo's younger sister is an eleven-year-old ball of massive energy and personality. She's confident and a bit reckless, and she often acts before she thinks. Izzie is always looking on the bright side, but she struggles to concentrate when dream crafting. She loves plushies and anime.

Logan

Mateo calls him a bully, Cooper calls him a friend, but either way, Logan is part of the dream chasers group. He doesn't have an hourglass like his friends to dream craft with, and he's not always the smartest, but when the crew is in a pinch, Logan does his best to help them out.

Lunia

One of the most powerful dream crafters to ever walk the dream world, Lunia managed to seal away the Nightmare King for a time and put the dream world at peace. Unfortunately, no one has seen her in years.

Mateo

Izzie's older brother is a quiet but very talented illustrator who spends most of his time doodling or working on his own comic book starring an imaginary character he created, called Z-Blob. Mateo is kind and incredibly creative, but he struggles with insecurity that holds him back from sharing his work with anyone for fear of criticism and rejection.

Mr. Guerrero

The art teacher at Mateo's school is a patient and insightful man who loves to guide and help future artists just like Mateo.

Mr. Oswald

Gruff but with a heart of gold, Mr. Oswald is a science teacher obsessed with space travel by day, and an expert dream crafter by night. He mentors and teaches the dream chasers to develop their dream crafting skills in order to protect the waking world and the dreamers from the dream world's nightmares.

Mrs. Castillo

This kind woman is like a grandma to the neighborhood, selling food and offering wisdom from her local food truck. She's a little odd, but some say the best people are.

Night Bureau

This secret organization maintains the balance between the waking and dream worlds and protects dreamers who might be in trouble.

Night Hunter

The Nightmare King's second-in-command is the ruthless and fearsome leader of the Nightmare Army. An expert archer and tracker, he captures dreamers all over the dream world to fulfill his master's will.

Nightmare King

He is the evil ruler of the Grim Realm—a dark corner of the dream world that is home to the collective fears and regrets of people's dreams—and cruel leader of the grimspawn hordes. The Nightmare King has escaped from his prison inside the Grim Realm, and now he is terrorizing sleeping kids and siphoning off their imaginations to fuel his Nightmare Army and change the dream world into a nightmare empire.

Riddle-Spokens

These powerful mythical beasts guard a special tower frequented in the Fantasy Realm. They're dangerous, and their riddles are tricky, but they tend to be good-hearted underneath.

Señor Tortuga

In the dream world, Mrs. Castillo's turtle, Señor Tortuga, becomes a traveling shop on four legs. He's a giant tortoise that carries Mrs. Castillo around, and the two of them always seem to appear just when you need them, despite Señor Tortuga's slow pace.

Sneak

This cat-like grimspawn has a devious mind and a lie waiting on his tongue at all times. He may be small, but he shouldn't be underestimated.

Snivel

If violence was the question, Snivel's answer would be yes. Built like a small knight, he bickers with Sneak and Susan just as much as they bicker with him.

Stone Golem

The second of the Riddle-Spokens is a giant made of stones with a lantern for a head. He tests the trespassers' fears, and if they don't pass, he is ready to deliver on his promise to throw them out the tower window.

Susan

This grimspawn has two horns to hold up her big attitude. She keeps Sneak and Snivel in line as the brains of the operation.

Waking world

This is the world that we know when we are awake.

Z-Blob

At first, Z-Blob was the main character of Mateo's comic book, but in the dream world, he came to life and become Mateo's faithful friend! Mateo loves to dream craft him into fierce warriors or vehicles. He is also the only dream creature who can cross into the waking world.

Zian
This strong blue cat-owl gryphon has mighty wings and acts as Zoey's loyal companion. She flies her around the dream world.

Zoey
Zoey is an aware dreamer who has already carved out a reputation in the dream world as the dream bandit foiling the Night Hunter's wicked plans. She prefers to work alone, but she often helps the dream chasers.

About the Author

Kaela Rivera is the award-winning author of the Cece Rios trilogy and currently lives in the soaring mountains of Utah. When she's not crafting stories, she's working as a managing editor for a marketing company—or secretly doodling her characters in the margins of her notebook. One of her greatest hopes is to explore the beauty of cultural differences and how they can bring us all closer.

Dream Journal

Dreams are like exciting adventures! But they quickly fade in the waking world. Use these pages to write down your dreams so you remember them when you return from the dream world.